we
hexed
the
moon

Mollyhall Seeley

WEATHERGLASS BOOKS

this one goes out to those teens in 2020 who tried to hex the moon.

jen

now.
new moon minus twelve hours

We hexed the moon, Maycie says.

Her hair is plastered to her face & drips onto Jen's floor as she climbs gracelessly through the window. It has been raining for days, a monsoon, the wettest August on record. Everything has been the -est on record. Hottest, coldest, wettest, driest, climate officially changed. Jen has spent all summer lost in social media timelines talking about dwindling glaciers, water wars are coming, who cares, it's hopeless, we've fucked it, we deserve whatever comes next. People throwing soup on art, like *that'll* do anything, why are we more upset about art than the ruined planet, blah & etc. Twitter is crumbling, fittingly, into a timeline of what are no longer called Tweets, now called Xs. Twitter is dead & so is nature, probably. Jen's never having kids. That's what Jen's college application essay was about, framed through a lens of climate grief, 'the sense of loss that arises from experiencing or learning about environmental destruction or climate change'. Jen's college counselor thought *grief* was a very powerful word. She said *Why say grief and not sadness* & Jen said *Sadness is local, grief is cosmic.* Global heating. Universal heating, maybe, who knows. So Jen's not having kids but she *is* going to Yale.

I know, says Jen, I was there. Also, why are you climbing through the window? My dad would have let you in. She finishes coming out of her bathroom, where she'd been trying to dig out a zit. The internet says never to try to erupt what's beneath the skin, doesn't do anything but make it worse. Probably true. But who cares, it's under her chin. Jen doesn't spend a lot of time looking up.

I couldn't have faced him, says Maycie, shuddering.

My dad? asks Jen. Why?

Because we *hexed* the *moon*, says Maycie again, more urgently this time. Jen leads her to the bed, sits her down. Grabs a slightly damp towel from the hamper & drops it over Maycie's head so she can dry her hair. She isn't even wearing a rain jacket, which: of course she isn't. Jen loves Maycie but she's never once made a sensible decision on purpose. Jen's always going to pick her up from places, reminding her when she's got projects due. Jen doesn't mind. Jen's good at that stuff. Plus Maycie's always been grateful, never forgets a thank-you, always writes really heartfelt birthday cards. Jen had written Maycie's college essay alongside her own, & Goldie's, but Harding hadn't let her. Maycie had said thank you & even given Jen some money for it but it was pointless in the end because Maycie had decided not to go to college for a while, which Jen strongly disapproved of, but Maycie said *Jen, we're not all geniuses like you*, & fair point, so Jen let it go.

I *know*, Jen repeats. Hard to forget. Plus it was yesterday.

Maycie ties her hair up in Jen's damp towel & glares. Her makeup is smudged at the corner of her eyes, making her look like she's been dragged from the water. She raises her arm

8

& points accusingly at Jen's window, mouth a furious line. *Listen*, dumbass, she demands, voice rising, almost hysterical now, but Maycie's always like that, easily ruffled. Jen's not. Jen's a pragmatist. Maycie finishes: You're not *listening!* I'm saying it *worked!*

Jen's gaze follows Maycie's outstretched arm. Through the open window & the branches of the tree just beyond, she can see the pitch-dark blanket of sky. The black of it trembles a little with stars, flickering like they're about to blow out. When she pokes her head outside, she sees that the stars are moving, drawn like gnats to a wound. Forming a circle. A big, empty circle, at the center of which should have been—

Maycie, says Jen.

I fucking *told* you, Maycie says.

The stars circle the nothingness like a hungry hollow mouth. In the center there is no moon.

yesterday.
(maycie)

Summer had come slow as honey and twice as sticky, dripping over the island like the afterthought of a particularly wet spring. The tides never seemed to go down all the way, and the edge of Maycie's yard was constantly murky with salt water that had climbed up over the retaining wall. The whole neighborhood hesitated to bring their boats out from the safety of the marinas, wary of storms. They were bad this year, worse than ever, thunder every day it seemed like. Maycie liked to sit on the covered porch and watch them roll over the water. There was a boat that had been abandoned and slowly sinking for most of Maycie's life and this was the spring that had finally done it, now nothing but a broken-off mast sticking up out of the water, sometimes a bird perched on it.

Anyway Goldie's parents didn't give a shit about their boat, and had docked it in early May. That's where they were now, the four of them spread out on the cushioned bow. Goldie was sunning herself, her pink bikini untied around the neck so she wouldn't get lines. She was glittering a little from generous application of coconut tanning oil. Fifteen minutes on her front, fifteen minutes on her back. Sunlight licking at her skin until it turned a dusky brown. Maycie looked at her body with a sort of sick feeling. Goldie didn't have an ounce of fat on her. She had an extremely delicate collarbone. Goldie was one of those people who moved differently, lithe, just looked good doing everything she did even if she was hunched over a computer or roasting herself like a stuck pig. Fifteen minutes and fifteen minutes. Even.

Dad said he was going to fish, Goldie explained about the boat. But personally I think they just wanted people to see the new paint job.

Maycie shifted her head. It was lying on Harding's crossed ankles, which were kind of digging into Maycie's temple. But she didn't want to move. She liked it. She squinted at Goldie, trying to find the outline of her in the late morning light. It was hard to make out; the glinting water behind her swallowed all her edges, blurring where she ended and the sunshine began.

Does your dad even fish?

Goldie shrugged.

Jen said, Also, the boat looks the same.

How dare you, Goldie gasped, hand clutching at her bare neck, pretending there were pearls pooled in the dip of her perfect collarbone. The boat is now aquamarine instead of teal.

Maycie's feet were in Jen's lap; Jen was wearing jeans. It was the hottest summer on record and Jen was wearing jeans like a sociopath. Maycie's hands twitched with the temptation to push her over the edge of the boat and into the water to cool her off. She'd jump in, too, after.

Can you tell me the substantive difference between aquamarine and teal, said Jen.

I dunno, said Goldie. Probably like ten grand?

Harding's fingers were tracing patterns on Maycie's bare shoulder. Maycie didn't think she was listening to this conversation about Goldie's dad's boat. What do *you* think? she asked Harding, rolling her head a little to make Harding pay attention.

I think Goldie should put a shirt on, Harding said. She's going to get burned.

I'm on a timer!

Jen snorted. Nice of you to evenly cook yourself so some sweaty ball-scratcher can jerk it to you on his Walmart NASCAR sheets.

Goldie sniffed. I'll have you know the guy I'm hooking up with does *not* have Walmart sheets. They're Egyptian cotton.

Hate to break it to you but you can buy Egyptian cotton sheets at Walmart, said Jen. Even *Max* has them. Just because it sounds foreign doesn't mean it's fancy. In fact with the globalization of the manufacturing market—

Okay, interrupted Goldie, okay, please, not this, it's summer I'm not sitting through an *economics lecture*—

I meant about the difference between aquamarine and teal, Maycie said to Harding, ignoring them. She was annoyed. She wished Harding wasn't looking at Goldie and paying attention to her skin. She knew Harding had known what she meant. She said: What's the difference, tell me.

The substantive difference?

Yeah.

Nothing. I think one is more blue than green and one is more green than blue. Dunno which is which. Harding's hand tightened a little on Maycie's shoulder; Jen and Goldie were still bickering.

Everybody shut up, said Harding, without raising her voice at all. She was still looking down at Maycie, and she'd gone back to drawing a design on Maycie's shoulder. Jen and Goldie both slumped a little and stopped bickering. Maycie felt something prickle underneath her skin, the instinct to act out, to not stop precisely because Harding had told her to. She'd never wanted to disobey, before. She'd liked it when Harding told her what to do, because it meant Maycie knew what the expectations were, and she could fulfill or even exceed them.

But that was before Harding had grabbed ahold of Maycie's shoulders in the scant, thin moonlight on a road without streetlights and kissed her so hard it felt like a bite on Maycie's lips. Now everything felt so upside-down that even when Harding gave clear instructions it felt like there was something hidden in them that Maycie didn't know how to answer.

But, Maycie protested, then stopped, gesturing at disobedience without performing it.

Harding bent down over her, bringing their faces closer. No, she said sharply. Let's eat.

Her bone structure was so stark in the morning light. Loose strands of hair framed her face despite the tight, sturdy knot Harding's impatient hands had tied. But they didn't soften the edge of Harding's jaw. The cut of her cheeks. The point of her chin.

Maycie looked away. She stood up. It was so bright, the sun so hot it hurt, Maycie's shoulders growing pink beneath the bite of it.

I'm not hungry, Goldie whined even as she followed Jen and Maycie to their feet, offering Harding a hand up. And everything's gonna be busy.

Mimi's won't, Jen offered, studiously checking her phone as if anybody would be texting her that wasn't on this boat. She just wanted to look nonchalant because she had a huge raging crush on the line cook there, some guy they'd gone to school with, though maybe he wasn't graduating, Maycie didn't remember the whole story but she thought maybe there was some drama about his credits. Or his grades. Or something about absences, whatever, she didn't really care. He had a six-pack and she never bothered to remember his name but Jen was always super drooly about him and pretended she wasn't because Jen thought she was above things like having a crush on people or even having any feelings at all.

Goldie and Maycie shared a look, and Maycie rolled her lips inward, trying not to laugh. Jen was so cute and *so* transparent, like a furious cat who refused to admit it wanted attention. Goldie hummed. I wonder who's on shift today, she mused, voice lilting and innocent.

Jen sniffed. How would I know? I'm not in charge of their shift schedule.

I hope it's Six-Pack, Maycie said, and danced away from where Harding tried to pinch her. He's so hot, don't you think, Jen? Maybe I'll give him my number.

Harding's second attempt at a pinch connected before

her hand flattened out on Maycie's waist and drew her in, guiding her to the edge of the boat. It was too hot to stand this close, but Maycie's skin under Harding's hand shivered. She didn't move away. Goldie cackled behind them, accepting Harding's other hand as she hopped from the boat onto the dock and scooped up the pile of towels, chucking them into the bin. Jen stood with her arms folded. Having unburdened herself, Goldie threw a glistening arm around Jen's shoulders. She looked so little in her swimsuit and her big glasses, hair a spinning wave down her back. She was so pretty that Maycie hated her sometimes. She felt herself take half a step closer toward Harding.

This is your hot girl summer, Jennypenny, I can feel it, Goldie cooed, and brushed a playful kiss to Jen's cheek. Last one before we all go off to college, you can finally let loose that wild party girl who lives inside you. No consequences! You never have to see any of these people again!

Jen shrugged her off. I'll have to see you idiots.

Goldie laughed, too loud as it echoed on the water. Well, yeah, of course you'll see *us*, she self-corrected, glancing at Harding and Maycie before bending down to pull her large white linen shirt over her head. *We're* going to be friends forever.

Harding's fingers toyed absently with the tag hanging out of Maycie's shorts. Her fingernails were blunt and soft against Maycie's skin. Two nights ago they'd been inside her, curling and uncurling like Maycie was being beckoned, drawn out from inside her body by Harding's hand. They were blunt and soft inside her, too. Maycie had never felt anything like it, not even the times she'd done it to herself. The first

15

time they'd done it, Harding had been shaking. She'd had her forehead pressed to Maycie's thigh, hard enough Maycie thought maybe there'd be a bruise. But there wasn't. Harding was going to Liberty University in the fall, Goldie to College of Charleston, Jen to Yale. Maycie was taking a year off and had so far made no plans except to buy a one-way ticket to Buenos Aires. She figured she could get there and then decide what came next. It felt too far away still to worry. It was only August.

I'm hungry, Maycie announced. Harding's fingers stilled. Maycie felt them stilling the same way she'd felt them moving. Let's go, okay? We'll go to Mimi's. She tangled her hand in Harding's and dragged her off the dock.

now.
new moon minus eleven and a half hours

Uh, Jen says. She pulls her head into the room. Sticks it back out again. Still the circle of stars. Still the nothing for them to circle. Maycie. Where the fuck is the moon.

WE *HEXED* IT, Maycie repeats, for what is now the third time. SO IT *DISAPPEARED*.

Jen sits down. The floor is hard. She's going to bruise. She says, But… the ocean. What about, like, tides? Climate grief, she thinks, somewhat hysterically.

Does it seem to you like I know anything about what happens to tides when the *moon disappears*? Maycie snaps, which Jen thinks is unfair, because Maycie has been given the benefit of time to process the disappearance of the moon & Jen is just learning about it. Also, it hadn't been Jen's idea to hex the moon in the first place. Jen doesn't even think witchcraft is *real*, she'd only gone along with the whole stupid thing because they'd had a good day, & Jen knows what she's like, okay. She knows she's bossy & a know-it-all & a little condescending, she can't help it, it's her personality. Why should she pretend to know less than she does? If her ideas & plans are the best ones why shouldn't they do them? But when yesterday they were all having fun & even Harding had wanted to do it Jen had been like, all right. Let's do a stupid little moon dance.

*No*body knows what happens to the tides when the moon disappears, Maycie is saying, because the moon has never disappeared before, because no one has ever hexed it! No one ever hexed the moon, Jen, in the entire history of the whole world, until *one* of us thought it would be *funny*—

Don't say it like that, like it was me, Jen tells her. Harding is the one who suggested it, *Harding* is the one who—

Ladies, says a soft voice. Jen shuts up. Jen shuts right up. The voice is melodic but layered, like four people talking all at once, none of them quite in sync, none of them quite harmonic. Ladies, please.

Jen & Maycie turn as one to stare at the door to Jen's bedroom, which has swung open. Standing half inside, half in the hallway, is… well. Jen blinks, then squints, then blinks again, but no, she's right. She's definitely right even though her brain is struggling to hold onto what she's looking at, which is, for lack of any better descriptors, the moon.

It's the fucking moon.

How does Jen know: she just does. *I think therefore I am.* Jen knows therefore she knows. It's the moon. The Moon. Doesn't look like a moon but has moon essence, if that's a thing that can be had, which it isn't, but then nor can the moon disappear from the sky & show up in somebody's bedroom, & yet. Here it is. She. It. She. Jen is trying to make this make sense, is still worrying sort of about the tides. Seasons. Nuclear autumn, but not nuclear. Cosmic. Cosmic autumn. Cosmic heating. Climate grief. Jen is possibly not going to Yale after all.

The Moon looks like – a woman, sort of. Almost. It looks like a woman the way a shadow does: Jen knows, in her brain, that it is a woman, it has the shape of a woman, but a woman lit up from the inside with a thin, pale light. Looking at her is somehow both soothing & unsettling, like when you take a selfie & the camera reverses your image. A camera filter that makes you old or young or a cartoon or Italian.

Holy shit you're The Moon, Maycie blubbers. Holy shit. Holy shit. The Moon. Holy shit.

Hm, says The Moon, her voices a lilt, the lilt a shiver down Jen's neck. The Moon steps more fully into the room, running her fingertips along the edge of Jen's dresser, scaring up dust. How interesting of you to use the word 'holy', now that I'm here in your bedroom, when yesterday I was – what was the phrase? – a 'fat old lady'.

This is Jen's bedroom, actually, Maycie tells The Moon, because Maycie is a spineless traitor. It's not her fault. Maycie's emotional. That's why she needs Jen so much, to be logical, the voice of reason. So Jen lets it go even though it actually is very messed up.

I know that, I'm the fucking moon, The Moon snaps at her. The crack of her voices makes the room shake, like literally shake; Jen has this fancy vase her mom bought off Instagram & it teeters *extremely* precariously on her bookshelf.

Maycie shrinks down. Sorry, she mutters, looking helplessly at Jen, who stands up & steps close to her & puts a soothing hand on her shoulder, because someone has to be calm & in charge & God knows it's not going to be Maycie.

19

The Moon smiles & the light inside her thins out, settling into a murky gray color. She *is* beautiful, Jen decides, in the sort of way that the view from a cliff's edge is beautiful. One time Jen's dad took them all to the Grand Canyon & their tour guide said *The demographic most at-risk here are males aged 18 to 24, they flirt too much with death*, & Jen's dad had joked *Hear that, Max? Watch your step.* Max didn't go to Yale. Max didn't go anywhere, is working as a bartender & living at home. Jen can't stop looking at The Moon, even though it gives her vertigo.

I can't believe it *worked*, Jen hears herself say, because this is the only thing she seems to be able to think for any extended period of time. So you're telling me magic is real and we're, like – can everyone do it, or are we special for some reason?

It didn't quote unquote 'work', The Moon tells her, disdainful, like Jen is the stupidest person in the room. It makes Jen feel like all the veins in her body are swelling up. Varicose, telangiectasia, venous thromboembolism. Related but not the same, Jen can tell you, Jen knows all the definitions. Venous thromboembolism is a fancy way to say a blood clot. Happens all the time, 600,000 instances per year in the United States alone. Can be bad. Can be nothing. Deep vein thrombosis is gentler than pulmonary embolism. Ask Jen something else. She can tell you. When Max's mom went to the hospital with a transient ischemic attack it was Jen who explained it to him, & yet The Moon thinks Jen is stupid. *The Moon* does. Jen is supposed to go to Yale in the fall, though with current events being what they are it seems more likely that nobody is going to college ever again. But the point stands that Jen had got in.

Anyway, Jen supposes, what did that matter to The Moon? The Moon says: You think four infants with the combined power of a chestnut are strong enough to hex The Moon out of the sky? Be reasonable, Jen.

I'm reasonable, says Jen. That's the number one thing I am.

Maycie is nodding, her obvious relief tumbling out of her in a whooshing sigh as she collapses back onto the bed. The towel unravels around her hair & lies limp as a wet worm on the bedspread. Of course, she says, of course, yeah. Obviously the hex didn't work, hexing the moon's not a thing.

Whether or not the hex worked isn't the *point*, The Moon corrects derisively. She clicks her fingernails against Jen's dresser & the wood cracks beneath her hand. She walks— walks? No, not really; moves somehow, impossibly, all at once but not like she's floating, more like she's in one place then another & another & it's like how the stars move in a time-lapse video. Her body moves so fluidly it's like she has no scaffolding. Jen feels the floor vibrate beneath her. Jen wants to watch it forever & also wants to close her eyes & never see it again; it hurts her head, trying to make it make sense.

The Moon crouches down in front of Jen & reaches out to twine her fingers into a strand of Jen's hair.

The point is that you tried to hex me in the *first* place, she continues, looking at Jen, breath sliding across Jen's face. It's cold. Space is cold, Jen knows that, space is freezing, gets colder the deeper you get. (Does The Moon have lungs?) I do nothing but help and what thanks do I get? Four pathetic morons trying to turn me into cheese. Do you even know what happens to cheese in space?

Jen & Maycie shake their heads in unison. Jen could make an educated guess based on what she knows about pressure & airlessness, but she doesn't want to get it wrong.

The Moon tuts quietly. Her grip on Jen's hair tightens. Jen wants to look to Maycie for help, but it feels sort of like if she looks away from the dark circles of The Moon's eyes, something terrible will happen, only she doesn't know what.

Nothing, probably, admits The Moon. But it can't keep your tides in check, I'll tell you *that* much.

The tides, yeah. Jen's been saying.

The Moon lets go of Jen's hair & drops so heavily onto Jen's floor that the house shakes. One of Jen's swimming trophies falls off the shelf above her bed, conking Maycie on the head, & when Maycie draws her hand away from the point of collision her fingers are wearing a coat of blood. Still: better that than the Instagram vase.

Oops, says The Moon, smiling a little, not sounding sorry. She sounds like Max when he says stuff like *What, so you think it's* good *we have all these Mexicans coming in and taking our jobs* & Jen says *What jobs Max, what job did they take from you* & he says *Don't be so literal Jen* & she says *Okay but there's literally people we need to hire to clean hospitals, are* you *taking that job* & he says *Not me but somebody American* & she says *You mean white* & he says *If that's how you want to define it*, like it's a trap, & Jen's mom says *Immigrants aren't all janitors Jen don't be racist* & Jen says *He just said Mexicans are stealing white people's jobs but I'm the racist?*

The Moon lets go of Jen's hair. Jen feels better, stops thinking about how much she hates Max & how pathetic her mother sometimes is about how much she wants Max to like her.

Downstairs, Jen's dad calls: Whoa! Was that an earthquake?

I'm looking on X right now, yells Max in answer. Max loves Elon Musk so Max loves X. He even remembers to call it X even though everybody else still says Twitter. He pays $8 a month to be verified. Horrific. Jen, Maycie, & The Moon look at one another. After a brief pause, a loud crashing sound comes from Max's room & then he is skidding into Jen's doorway, pale. Jen, he says, breathless. Jen. The moon.

Jen glances over at The Moon, who shrugs, looking delighted.

I can explain, Jen begins, despite having absolutely no idea how.

You can explain that the MOON HAS DISAPPEARED? Max is looking at Jen, not at The Moon. Not even at Maycie even though Jen knows he thinks Maycie is hot. He thinks Goldie is the hottest but everyone thinks that. Maycie he likes because he says she has Wife Potential.

He can't see me, The Moon explains cheerfully. This is strictly a *you* problem, babe.

You meaning Jen? *You* meaning Jen & Maycie? *You* meaning the four of them?

What are you doing just standing there? Max snaps, like there's some obvious thing Jen is supposed to be doing, like there's an Absent Moon Protocol that she's somehow missed even though between the two of them Jen's the one who actually *reads*. DAD. DAD, X SAYS THE MOON IS GONE. THE EARTHQUAKE WAS BECAUSE THE MOON IS GONE.

Well, he's not *wrong*, muses The Moon. Anyway, there *might* be earthquakes. Hard to say. I've never disappeared before.

What do you mean 'the moon is gone'? Jen's dad asks, appearing behind Max in the doorway. Oh, hi, Maycie. Didn't hear you come in.

Used the window, Maycie explains, a little breathlessly. Because of The Moon. It's, uh. She glances at The Moon, who crosses her legs (legs?) & gives a smug little wave. Well, it's not in the sky anymore.

Jen's dad frowns. Is this one of those internet things?

The Moon is very real, says Maycie. We have a very real and literal problem with the very real and literal Moon.

Max holds up his phone. Fox News is reporting that the moon is… maybe it was knocked out of orbit? But some of the guys I follow are suggesting it might be spontaneous combustion. People are *freaking out*.

Are these guys scientists or just dudes who bought NFTs, Jen asks, can't help herself. Maycie elbows her side; Jen knows this is not the time to pick a fight with Max, but she can't always control it, the stuff that comes out of her mouth.

The moon is made out of rocks, rocks don't spontaneously combust, says Jen's dad, taking Max's phone with a frown & moving toward the window. What kind of— holy shit, the moon is gone!

I *told you*!

Jen holds her hands out, climbing to her feet. The Moon thinks Jen is stupid but Jen's not, Jen's 'eminently pragmatic', it says so in her guidance counselor case file. Okay, she says, okay, let's calm down. I'm sure The Moon will be back soon.

She looks meaningfully at where The Moon is reclining. The Moon snorts. Fat chance, Jennifer, she says. Enjoy your six hours of daylight and nonexistent seasons. Or possibly extreme seasons. Who knows.

Maycie lets out a wailing sound & buries her face in her hands. We're fucked! We fucked it! We totally fucked everything!

There must be a reasonable explanation for this, Jen's dad mutters, doubtfully. A scientific one.

X says it might be a government conspiracy to keep us complacent now that the COVID conspiracy has been debunked, says Max. But also some people on Reddit are saying it was a *spontaneous dissolution event.*

The COVID conspiracy, Jen repeats. You don't believe that. Not even Max was stupid enough. Max had gotten all his vaccine shots, even the boosters, & to Jen's knowledge hadn't even complained about it.

I'm just reporting both sides, Max says. I didn't make the Xs, I'm just reading them.

The Moon didn't dissolve, and it's not a conspiracy, Jen tells him. She isn't going to panic. She isn't. Jen is reasonable. *Eminently.* Pragmatic & sound of mind. That was her college essay, not letting climate grief stop you from trying to make change. Be practical & don't have kids til you know they're inheriting a better world. Or whatever. Magic is just science nobody understands yet. There has to be something, some explanation, some way to put it all back. Some way to undo it. There has to be some way to fix what has erupted in Jen's bedroom, the Moon's delicate toes wiggling, her smile a wicked curl, as she watches Jen try to hold the world in place.

Then where did it go? snaps Max. Since you know everything?

Jennifer, Jennifer, echoes The Moon's voice in her head, singsong. *What's a clever girl to do? Hm?*

Jen looks helplessly at The Moon, who isn't smirking per se but gives the impression of smirking, or perhaps of having smirked. Tell them I'm on vacation, The Moon says, & when she laughs it makes the whole room shake.

yesterday.
(goldie)

Mimi's was small, just four booths and a handful of seats at the diner counter. It was cash only, which was truly wild, in Goldie's opinion, because it was 2023 and literally *who* carried cash anymore, especially after the pandemic? Like, thank God they had the sense to at least have their own ATM, though it charged four actual dollars to make a withdrawal, which was probably a war crime, and Maycie swore that one time she saw a cockroach climb out of the money mouth. Gross. Fucking *gross*. Goldie would swear to God it was getting smaller on the inside every time she came in.

But it was cheap. So.

Maycie flung herself into the booth seat closest to the window and dragged Harding down beside her, as if this were at all a subtle gesture. Goldie rolled her eyes in Jen's direction and Jen shot her a look of weary solidarity back. It had been a year and a half of this nonsense, Maycie and Harding glancing at one another and pretending to do a normal amount of touching. As if Harding *ever* did a 'normal' amount of touching. Before Henry died, he and Goldie once spent a whole week at Harding's house because Harding's mom had freaked out when she learned they were staying at the house alone while their parents were on vacation to Morocco. In that time Harding had held Goldie's hand exactly *zero* times. They'd shared a bed and Harding hadn't even let Goldie snuggle her! She said it was too hot!

Jennnnnn, go get the menus, Goldie whined, dropping into the seat across from Harding and Maycie and stretching her legs out along the bench so there was no room for Jen to sit.

I know what you're doing, Jen informed her, unimpressed, but went to get the menus anyway, just like everyone knew she secretly wanted to. Goldie *had* to do these things or Jen would die virginal and tragic.

Harding was giving Goldie that patented Disapproving Dad look. Be *nice*, Goldie, Jesus.

I'm *being* nice! Goldie protested, gesturing at where Jen was leaning over the counter, looking too-casual as Six-Pack bent over to pick up some menus from beneath her. She had her fucking *book* out on the counter, God, Goldie loved her to pieces but she was so massively embarrassing all the time. I'm *telling* you, if someone doesn't force her to talk to him, she'll never do it.

Why does she have to talk to him? Harding returned, voice bland. He sucks.

Goldie sighed heavily. Harding didn't get it, which wasn't a surprise. Like, yeah, Six-Pack did happen to suck, but there were plenty of nice dudes if only you were willing to, you know, *be nice* to them, which Jen typically wasn't, so Jen was going to have to make do with a guy who would think her snottiness was flirting.

So her taste is bad, Goldie agreed with a shrug. She'll live and learn.

Maybe he has hidden depths, Maycie offered, conciliatory.

He doesn't, Goldie said. Hardyparty's right, he sucks. Also, Liz Harrison says he's bad at kissing. She says he uses, and I'm quoting, 'too much mouth'.

Maycie let out a peal of laughter, loud enough that several people at the counter and an entire booth turned to glare at her. Goldie felt the attention on the back of her shoulders like a sunburn. She liked it when they looked and she didn't like it. It made Goldie feel good, that they looked at her, that they couldn't look away. But she didn't want to be looked at. She wanted them to have to look at her but she didn't want them to *be looking at her*, if that made any sense.

Screw them, anyways, Goldie thought; they could laugh if they wanted. There weren't quiet hours at Mimi's, and anyway, it was 11 a.m.

Who cares if a shitty knockoff Paul brother is bad at kissing, Jen's not going to kiss him, Harding said as Jen slid back into the booth beside Goldie, tossing the menus and her book on the table. *The Book of Disquiet*. God, fucking *Jen*.

Maycie snorted into her hand. Oh my God he *does* look like a Paul brother.

Who? asked Jen, as if she didn't know. Goldie nestled up beside her, apologetic in her affection, resting her head on Jen's shoulder. Jen let her but didn't bring a hand up to scratch through Goldie's hair, which meant she was mad Goldie made her go to the counter but she felt bad about it. So that was fine. Jen had her moods but she burned through them pretty quick.

Six-Pack, Goldie told her.

He doesn't look like a *Paul brother*, Jen said, appalled.

Blond, said Harding flatly, ticking off on her fingers. Square but not thick. Terrible chin. Nasal voice. Mouth does that weird thing where his lips thin out when he thinks he's making a joke.

Maycie nodded so fervently her hair bounced. Also: not funny, but I guess that's not really a physical trait.

Who cares? It's not Six-Pack's *funny* bone Jen wants to examine, Goldie said, raising her head so she could wave a dismissive hand and give Jen an obnoxious wink.

Oh my *God*, Jen muttered, dropping her head onto the table with a thump. I'm not going to date the *diner guy*, okay? He literally took remedial Algebra *twice*.

Goldie took Jen's head between her palms and dragged her up, forcing their eyes to meet. Jennifer, first of all, you are not going to date Six-Pack because he's a boring shithead, and I won't allow it. You're just gonna bone. Secondly, and I mean this, if you administer an AP exam to every dude you wanna hump, you're going to be a virgin forever.

Plus, hot-but-stupid is very in right now, Maycie added, emptying a salt pack onto the table and pushing her finger into it. That's my niche.

Incorrect, Harding said.

Maycie pulled a dramatic face. Why!

Jen sighed. Harding, tell Maycie you think she's hot before she makes a scene and they refuse to serve us breakfast.

Goldie elbowed her. Just because Jen was mad at Goldie didn't mean she had to take it out on Maycie and Harding.

Jen elbowed back, a little meanly, and then both of them turned to look expectantly at Harding, who was staring at the table with her mouth in a flat line.

Maycie knows what she looks like, Harding snapped, before grabbing a menu and disappearing behind it.

Jen winced. *Sorry*, she mouthed across the table, and Maycie pretended not to know what she was talking about by busily announcing that she wanted pancakes, at least six of them, and a heaping side of fried green tomatoes.

I'll share with you, Jen offered, an apologetic gesture if Goldie ever saw one. And we can get milkshakes, too.

Maycie grinned. Deal.

Jen struck out her hand, and Maycie took it. Goldie nudged Harding's shin underneath the table until she muttered Bacon and egg sandwich for me. No milkshake. Goldie herself just ordered a soda with lemon. Goldie wasn't hungry a lot of the time. She wanted to be hungry but it was like her body didn't want food. She forgot about it all the time, until suddenly she'd realize she was nauseous and felt faint and that her hands were shaking, and then she'd go into the kitchen and shovel whatever nonpoisonous thing she could get her hands on into her mouth, just to get it over with.

When Goldie turned back to the table, Harding had put the menu down, and the three of them were building some kind of structure using only salt packets. Jen was saying something stern about structural integrity, and Maycie was laughing about it hard enough to make the whole structure wobble and fall.

now.
new moon minus eleven hours

Jen's dad disappears into his office to call Jen's mom, who is still in Oklahoma with Jen's grandparents because her grandfather had to get hearing aids put in & Jen's mom is one of those people who worries about everything & always has to be involved. Jen's mom is a highly emotional person. Max is growing roots on the couch in front of the TV, splitting his attention between cable news & the internet, which is tearing itself apart trying to decide what had happened to the moon. Jen's briefly glad she lives on an island where the worst thing anyone can really do is loot boutique stores or the Publix.

Dad, we're going to Goldie's, Jen yells on their way out the door. Call me if the moon comes back.

Beside her, The Moon gives her a very dry look, but fuck The Moon, Jen is beginning to suspect that The Moon is a huge dick. Or – Divine Feminine; The Moon is a huge cunt? Jen doesn't know. Jen's aware of the discourse. Jen's trans-inclusive.

Her dad pokes his head out of the office, frowning. Should you be going anywhere? he asks. The moon is gone and Max's internet friends say it's getting chaotic out there. I'm not sure if we should leave the house.

Yeah, The Moon croons, draping her arms over Jen & Maycie's shoulders, hanging her head low between them & twisting her neck at a nearly impossible angle so she can flutter her eyelashes. Some assholes hexed the moon, Jen.

The Moon's grip on Jen's shoulder is almost enough to break a bone, or feels like it anyway, & Jen recalls The Moon is essentially a big piece of debris from a planet that collided with earth billions of years ago & got stuck in earth's gravitational pull. The planets' cores fused, which explains why earth's core is so big. The planet was called Theia. Greek for divine, sometimes called Euryphaessa, 'wide-shining'. Anyway, the planets collided head-on & Theia's remains are partly on earth somewhere, swallowed up, & partly out in space, as the moon. So Jen's not sure why she's acting like she's top banana. If anything, earth won that particular collision. I lived bitch dot meme.

This guy on Reddit who says he works for NASA is hypothesizing that the earth could be the next planet to have a spontaneous dissolution event, Max calls from the living room, & Jen's dad says, Right. That's it. You're staying here. If we dissolve, we're dissolving together.

Even me? Maycie asks.

Jen's dad hesitates, then says, I mean. You're always welcome, Maycie, but you should ask your mom.

She and Rick are in Boulder at the Festival of Mother Gaia, Maycie says. It's just me at home.

Then yes, decides Jen's dad. You too. You can dissolve with us.

We're not going to *dissolve*, mutters Jen. This is so stupid.

The fucking *moon* is gone, snaps Max from the couch. What, you wanna dissolve with some other family?

First of all, yeah, literally *any* other family, Jen sneers, & The Moon laughs, a pleased tumble of off-pitch musical notes. Jen doesn't know why Max is even acting like he cares since all he ever does is repeat ignorant shit from the internet & make sure Jen knows she was conceived while their dad was still married to Max's mom, like that's Jen's fault. Jen's not the one who's always saying hateful political stuff specifically to hurt her mom's feelings & make their dad angry. *Jen* knows how to be civilized.

And secondly, Jen goes on, fuck off. You never clear your internet history and I'll tell everyone in this house right now what your last pre-Moon Google search was, I swear to God.

Max is looking at her with an expression of real horror on his face & Jen's thinking, like, good. Fuck you. You think I don't know what kind of person you are? You think I still look up to you? You still live at home. I'm going to *Yale*.

When Jen was little, she'd adored Max. She'd followed him around everywhere. She thought he was the cleverest, funniest, strongest, coolest, & best big brother that it was possible to have, & he'd loved her at some point too. But then he'd found out – somehow; Jen never asked – about how Jen came to be conceived, about Jen's mom's job as a tennis pro at their dad's golf club & long nights where their dad stayed late to 'practice'. Well: Jen's not one to cry over spilled milk. But there was something uniquely horrible about the first time she broke into Max's computer & saw all the shit he was watching on YouTube, about realizing Max wasn't saying all that dumbfuck

34

right-wing shit to mess with her, or at least not *just* to mess with her. She'd read all about it, the radicalization of young men online. Ben Shapiro, incels, the manosphere, all that shit. Fine. The internet was for porn, politics & hate crimes, everybody knew that; if you couldn't handle it then you didn't belong there. Jen herself was practical, it didn't bother her except as a logistical problem. Progress always came with backlash. You couldn't flinch from it, it was happening & always happened so you just had to look at it & keep looking. Whatever. It's just that she'd believed it was real but not that it would happen to Max. She'd thought Max was too stupid for radicalization. She didn't know Max would, like. Deliver on praxis.

The worst part was that Jen kind of saw his point about her mom. Jen was glad to be alive, but you'd have to be stupid not to realize her mom had lifted her skirt on a tennis court for someone who was paying for her time. That was something Jen had said once during a fight & things had never really gone back to normal – her mom had said Jen needed to get a summer job & Jen said, *How's sex work sound?* & her mom said, *Excuse me?* & Jen said, *You know, like you did, when you met Dad. How were the tips?* & then Jen's mom had burst into tears, her mom was *always* bursting into tears, it was exhausting, & Jen's dad had yelled but Max had been startled into laughter, real genuine laughter, delight on his face, & he'd said, *Jenny oh my God.* For a second Jen had felt like maybe it was us-against-them again, just for a second, her & Max, but then she remembered that his laughter was calling Jen's mom a slut, & Jen could do it, but fuck Max if he wanted to, so she'd flipped him off & stormed out.

Jen's dad points a stern finger at her. No one is leaving the house. If you want to see your friends and their parents are comfortable with *them* walking around in a world without a moon, that's their business. I'm still trying to get ahold of your mom, but all the phone lines are crashing.

At least Jen's grandma is too crazy to realize she's going to die in a spontaneous dissolution event, Max mutters.

Don't call her crazy, Jen's dad says.

Why? She is, just like Jen's gonna be. Sad.

Wow, hard to believe you wanna dissolve with a different family, The Moon muses. Jen feels gratified; everyone is always like, *Don't let him get to you*, but The Moon gets it. The Moon unwinds herself from Jen & Maycie & walks over to where Max is seated on the couch. She tilts her head at him, humming thoughtfully, like a cat observing a bug it has not yet decided to eat.

Jen watches in a kind of trance as The Moon lays a heavy hand on Max's chest & slowly presses her weight down on it. Max coughs, then rubs over where her hand is, not noticing it. He coughs again, tries to sit up, can't. His breath begins to come out in a wheeze. Jen is thinking about how the moon's surface gravity is one-sixth of the earth's, which in theory should make her not very heavy all shrunk down, when you think about it, unless she's *still* one-sixth of the earth's gravity, like if it didn't diminish along with her size, even though it should have, right? In theory?

The Moon keeps pushing down, expression curious, smile faint, like she doesn't know what could happen if she keeps pushing down, if she pushes & doesn't stop, if her hand goes into his chest & then through it, bloodied on the couch cushions beneath him.

The Moon looks up at Jen, grin flickering. *Easy peasy*, her voice in Jen's head hums. *Isn't it? Just to stand there and let me solve your problems?*

Max's last internet search was *virgin first time rough sex raw secret*. The video he'd watched was 'DON'T GET CAUGHT / FUCKING MY LITTLE SISTER'S VIRGIN BEST FRIEND RAW ON MY SISTER'S BED'. Jen knows this because he'd looked it up on his iPad & then left his iPad on the couch & Jen knows that his password is his birthday because Jen is brilliant & Max is a complete moron, amazing they share any DNA at all & that the DNA they share is in fact the smart DNA because her dad is the one with the PhD in philosophy & her mom graduated with a bullshit degree in English from some dinky college in New England nobody's ever heard of, not even Jen, & she's *seen* the diploma.

Anyway: Max sucks & doesn't love her anymore, but he's her half-brother. She's not… it wouldn't be right to let… she hates him but she doesn't want him *dead*. That would be psychotic, or not psychotic, Jen's trying not to use medical terms as insults because it's ableist now. Jen's not thinking about letting The Moon murder Max but there's a part of her, okay, yes, that likes watching him suffer a little bit. *Virgin first time rough sex raw secret. Fuck you. Fuck you.*

Jen says, You've made your point! Stop! & when The Moon looks up at her, she's laughing.

Ahhh, Jennifer, close call, The Moon tuts into her brain as she withdraws her hand. Max breathes.

The Moon sighs, unpeeling herself from the back of the couch where she is still looming over Max. Maycie's nails are digging trenches into Jen's skin. The Moon walks past them both without looking at them, voice bored when she reaches the foot of the steps & purrs, Well? Come on, ladies. Looks like we'll need to have our little sleepover here.

Jen & Maycie follow after her, Maycie already on her phone, typing to the group chat that Jen's dad had vetoed anyone leaving the house because of the moon thing. *ALSO, we have the moon, and the moon says this whole thing is our fault. double also she just tried to kill max i think*

Jen's at the base of the stairs when Max grabs her arm. Maycie keeps on ahead of her but Jen waits. Don't tell, Max says, eyes darting away. You shouldn't have gone on my iPad. That's an invasion of privacy.

Whatever, Jen says, turning away. You're disgusting, what else is new.

Max doesn't let go of her arm. Look, it's not real.

Jen rolls her eyes. She knows how the argument works. All language is ableist, all people are bad, everything is a crisis always, what's the point? Throw soup on art. Don't have kids. She says: Look, just leave my friends out of your rape fantasies, thanks.

Key word *fantasy*, Max says. Aren't feminists supposed to love porn now? If I didn't look at it someone else would. Or wouldn't, and then they wouldn't make any money. It's better to have this job than no job.

I'm familiar with the Catch-22, says Jen.

Goldie texted back! Maycie yells down the stairs. Jen

checks her phone. In the group chat Goldie has said *bitch the fuck u mean u 'have the moon'*

i mean we have the moon, Maycie answers, & sends a snap of The Moon flicking Jen's mom's porcelain horse statue off its place of honor at the top of the stairs. The house shakes again & Max yells out, voice sore-sounding, as one of the fancy lamps rattles its way off the side table. There's going to be no glassware left in Jen's house.

Jen abandons Max downstairs, not looking back. When her phone rings she answers by saying, I know what you're about to say and I don't know what to tell you. It's the fucking Moon.

Did you guys do drugs or something, Goldie demands as Maycie, Jen, & The Moon squeeze back into Jen's room. Jen closes the door, locking it. It can't be the *moon*, what are you talking about?

Hexing The Moon was *your* dumb idea, Jen snaps back. You're the one with the *Google-sourced* ritual and the lack of impulse control—

Put her on speaker, says The Moon. So Jen puts the phone on speaker. Hello, Golden. The Moon's voice is layered again, melodic. Jen hadn't noticed it becoming more normal until the layers came back. She wonders if The Moon even knows she's doing it. So lovely to finally speak to you in person. It's me, The Moon.

What the fuck, Goldie laughs. You're not the *moon*. We didn't *hex* the *moon*, you can't hex the *moon*, it's *the moon*.

That's not what you said yesterday when you were drawing a pentagram in Maycie's Winter Room and shouting at me

39

in Latin, The Moon croons. Then her mouth curls around a smile. That's not what you said when you were begging me to keep your secrets. When you were thinking that if the man in the moon were a lady, she had fat cheeks.

The line goes quiet. For a long time, Goldie says nothing. Then: How… how did you know I was—

I'M THE FUCKING MOON, shouts The Moon, & shoves the phone back to Jen, apparently finished with the conversation.

Please come over, Jen mutters weakly into the phone, just before Goldie hangs up.

yesterday.
(harding)

They were at Maycie's house, because Maycie's mom was gone, the only parent who regularly was. Harding's parents certainly never were: Harding's parents didn't believe in unsupervised youth. They thought that was where bad things crept in, sin and lust and. And. Meanwhile Maycie's mom went to the Gaia Festival in Boulder every July and ever since Maycie hit fifteen she'd left her at the big plantation-style house alone. Maycie's mom said its quirks made it 'spiritual' and Goldie said they made it 'fucking haunted'. It was true that the whole building had something oozing about it. But Harding didn't believe in ghosts. Harding didn't believe, generally. Ghosts, spirits. Crystals. The universe. The future. God: maybe. Undecided. Sometimes so much she felt paralyzed by it. The All of it. The Everything. But sometimes not at all. That felt big in a different way. Blazing.

The house's paint peeled in strange places, no matter how many refresher coats Maycie's mom had plastered on, and the more they added the worse it drooped as it grew heavier and heavier. The wood went soft and bendy when the weather changed. There was a room upstairs you could only get into through the window during summer, because the wood swelled in the heat and locked it shut. They called it the Winter Room. Maycie used to have nightmares that she'd get stuck up there in February and die, slowly, of hunger and boredom. She'd told Harding this while curled up beside her, naked, legs entwined. Harding's whole body had been vibrating with, she didn't know, maybe terror. That's how it always felt with Maycie. Harding's brain gone quiet, Harding just a body and its functions.

Now Maycie was laughing, her hair a soft halo around her head, framed by the sun. It made her whole body shine, a light dark thing, in sharp contrast to the faded baby pink of her T-shirt.

Harding's hands connected with Maycie's back in a soft catch, the pull of the swing stirring up the smell of whatever the magenta-flowered trees were that grew alongside Maycie's yard. Harding stepped back and then pushed forward again, sending Maycie back toward the light.

From the porch, Goldie waved two glasses with blood-colored liquid in them, the ice rattling like loose teeth. Get it while it's cold! she yelled. If the ice melts it'll get all watery.

Coming! Maycie called back, but made no motion to slow the arc of her swing. Harding would have to stop her. The problem was that Harding never *wanted* to stop her; that the thing on the tip of Harding's tongue was always shaped like *yes*.

Four months ago, Maycie had walked Harding home in the reedy moonlight, talking about Harding didn't know what. She had been busy trying to keep all the things she wanted from spilling out over her teeth. Maycie had stopped walking, breathless with whatever careless thing she was saying, shoulders soft in the white light of the sky above them, and Harding's dad said a man without self-control is like a city broken into and left without walls. Proverbs 25:28. Sometimes Harding felt like a jar whose lid kept rattling, whose fermented insides were threatening to shatter the glass.

Harding? Maycie had asked, head tilting to the side, braid tumbling from her shoulder. You coming, or?

Harding had closed her eyes and grabbed onto Maycie's shoulders and pressed their lips together. Maycie had made a sound Harding had never heard before as she flung her arms around Harding's shoulders and clung like someone was going to try to pull her away.

Now, Harding caught the swing rope and jogged backward, slowing it to a stop. Maycie looked over her shoulder, pouting a little.

You're beautiful, Harding had thought, and hadn't been able to say, at the diner. Smart funny soft, the inside of you is warm, the outside of you is warm I want to touch you all the time I want to know what you feel like every second. Proverbs 25:28.

Ice'll melt, Harding said.

Maycie sighed, hopping off the swing and wobbling a little on the landing, hand darting out to Harding's shoulder until she steadied. They walked together to the porch, wrists brushing, not quite holding hands. Goldie was stretched out on the wicker love seat, sunning herself again. She was taking a selfie, twisting her midriff until it pulled at her skeleton, collarbone jutting out.

There she is, Goldieboldie, our beautiful roast duck, Maycie teased, nudging Goldie's stomach with her foot.

43

Nice and crispy, Goldie agreed without looking away from her phone. Hey, which one of these is better?

Maycie snatched the phone from her hand so she and Jen could bend their heads over it, scrolling. Harding didn't look. Harding didn't have social media; not allowed. Her dad trusted her not to lie, so he didn't check her phone. Harding did, though. Lie, that is. She'd gotten very good at it.

This one, Maycie decided. It looks more candid.

It's a selfie, Maceface, by definition it cannot be candid, corrected Jen. But yeah, that's the best one.

Goldie took her phone back, smacking her lips cheerfully. Sun's out guns out, she said as she wrote. Sun emoji, moon emoji, peace emoji, we out.

Leave the moon out of this, Maycie laughed, taking a long sip of her drink and then making a face. Jesus, what's in this?

Booze, sugar, and lemon, Jen explained, voice dry. She put like nine different types of juice in it. Why does your mom even have all that juice.

They were doing a cleanse before the festival, to ready their bodies and spirits for Mother Gaia, Maycie said with a shrug, *they* being Maycie's mom and her new boyfriend, Rick, who vaped inside and called Harding by her first name.

Jen snorted, then dodged Maycie's hand when it came out to hit her in reproach. Sorry, sorry. I respect your mom's weird hippie religion as much as I respect Harding's.

So, not at all, Goldie surmised. Harding stirred the liquid in her glass and said nothing. 2 Corinthians 4:4: The god of this world has blinded the minds of the unbelievers, to keep

44

them from seeing the light of the gospel of the glory of Christ, who is the image of God.

Harding felt her mouth twist.

I'm just saying, it's as equally possible that there's some creepy old man in the sky who watches our every move as it is that the moon needs a bunch of old hippies to have sex in a field in order for it to turn the tides, or whatever.

Maycie sighed. Harding knew she didn't put much stock in her mother's particular belief set, but there was something about the smug way Jen talked about it that always made her want to argue. Harding learned a long time ago that the best way to make Jen shut up was to simply look at her and wait; but Maycie didn't have Harding's patience.

Okay, so first of all, Mother Gaia is the *earth*, she said, the *moon* is the Divine Feminine, which is like, a totally different thing—

Two fake things don't make one real thing, said Jen.

Wow, Jen, said Goldie in the voice she used only when she wanted to be annoying. I can't believe you don't believe *the moon* exists.

Yeah, like, believe science, Jen, added Maycie.

You guys are assholes, said Jen, visibly struggling not to lose her cool. You know I believe *the moon exists*, you know that's not what I'm saying—

That night four months ago, the moon on Maycie's shoulders had been soft and tempting, rippling like silk. Harding hadn't been able to keep from touching it. Had put her hand into its light and watched it pool around her fingers, welcoming and cold.

45

My dad says all that stuff is real, Harding heard herself say, the Gaia stuff, and that it's satanic.

Your dad says there's a dude in the sky who once gave a man super strength through the power of his braids, said Jen.

The man in the moon is the deeeeevil, Goldie sang, badly.

No, the moon is feminine, and Satan is absolutely a dude, Maycie insisted through a laugh, and hiked her feet up into Harding's lap. Harding felt helpless to do anything other than bring her hands up to wrap around them, keeping them secure. (Her dad said Luke 6:46: Why do you call me 'Lord, Lord', and not do what I tell you?) She squeezed and let go. She wanted to bite them, to taste Maycie's skin in her mouth.

There's the other one that's evil, that's a lady. Harding, you know what I'm talking about.

Lilith, Harding said. But it's not really – that's kind of a misconception. Most translations don't mention her by name, she's just a night demon who comes out during the waning moon to seduce men.

Good for her, said Goldie. That's hot girl shit.

Maycie's foot twitched in Harding's grip. Moon's waning now, I think. Dost thou wish to live deliciously? she crooned, and Harding thought, yes. Harding was always thinking yes and saying no, Harding was always standing there with her heart in her mouth, refusing to open her lips.

Something was fermenting inside her and shattering beneath her skin, and Harding said: Let's try.

Goldie, Jen, and Maycie turned as one to look at her, expressions identical.

Come again? said Jen.

You think all the spiritual stuff is bullshit, Harding pointed out, letting her tone be a challenge, letting her words get under Jen's skin. So let's like – let's do one of Maycie's mom's rituals. If you're right, nothing will happen. And if you're not... She shrugged.

Nothing would happen. Harding wasn't sure she believed in demons any more than she believed in the image of God that hung in the center of her mother's cross collection, but something clawed its way up her throat anyway. Something hungry. Something greedy that said *yes*, said *do it*, said *that's hot girl shit*.

Said *if nothing happens, then your father is wrong*.

Wrong about the devil. Wrong about who knew what else.

... Okay, so, just to be clear, Reverend Church Camp over here is suggesting we do witchcraft to summon a moon demon? Jen said, gesturing between herself and Harding.

If it's fake, why does it matter? Harding returned. Unless you're worried it'll work?

I'm not worried it'll *work*, Jen snapped, I'm *worried* you're having a psychotic *break*.

Maycie pulled her feet from Harding's lap and tucked them under the seat cushion. She was looking at Harding with an expression Harding couldn't read. She said tentatively, like she wasn't sure whether she was taking seriously something that was meant to be a joke: My mom has... like, candles and herbs and stuff. They're in the basement, I think. But I don't know any of the like – she waved a vague hand in the air – rituals.

47

Goldie sat up. This is the best day of my life, she announced, thumbing open her phone. Hold on, hold the *fuck* on, I'm gonna look up what to do. There's definitely a tutorial somewhere, witches on Tumblr *love* to talk about their quote unquote craft.

This is *so* dumb, Jen told them. This is the dumbest shit.

Shut up, Jen, Goldie snapped. Harding's being cool for the first time in her extremely tragic life. Do *not* ruin this for me.

I think Harding's always cool, Maycie protested loyally, glancing at Harding and then away.

Thank you, said Harding.

Maycie shrugged. Jen pinched the bridge of her nose. Goldie looked up from her phone and chirped, Okay! I found one! Oh my God this is gonna be so fucking dope, we're gonna need a *teaspoon* of *blood*, and Harding remembered that James 5:12 said let your yes be yes.

now.

new moon minus ten and a half hours

Maycie paces back & forth, nervously twisting her hair, which hasn't finished drying. In all the hubbub Jen forgot: it had rained. Wettest spring, hottest summer, etc. Climate grief. Crazy that you can develop a whole psychological condition around just finding out that the earth is dying. Not crazy: ableist again. Supposedly. Jen read that you're supposed to say 'wild' now but then someone else said 'wild' was anti-Indigenous. So she doesn't know. Maybe no such thing as the right word. Maybe all words are bad, everybody give up. Jen's mom was complaining about the cost of healthcare right when her granddad's implant stuff was happening & Jen said *At least you guys will get Medicare it'll be gone by the time I'm old* & her mom had said *Oh Jen don't be such a pessimist* & Jen said *I'm not I don't plan to let it impact me* & her mom said *What do you mean?* & Jen said *I'm gonna die in the water wars like everybody else. Duh.*

Die sooner, said Max.

Kill yourself, said Jen.

Kids Please, said their dad.

Harding watches Maycie with her usual half-lidded gaze, cross-legged on Jen's bed with Jen's stuffed corgi pillow on her lap, fingers twisting its ears. Jen resists the urge to tell her to stop because she'll stretch them out of shape. Harding hasn't looked at The Moon basically at all, has just looked at Maycie this whole time. Goldie says they're in love but Jen thinks that's bullshit. They're eighteen. *Virgin first time rough sex raw secret.* That's how people *are.* Jen doesn't get it but she knows it's true.

From the floor, where she had flopped unceremoniously upon arrival, Goldie is staring up at The Moon, chin in her hands. She is wearing a silk pajama set & a pair of army boots that had definitely belonged to poor Henry because they're like four sizes too big. Jen's above trying to look sexy when she sleeps, that's some real body horror shit, Jen wouldn't buy sexy pajamas even if they were comfortable. On principle. Anyway when Goldie had come in Max had looked up from the TV & given her a smarmy look & drawled, Looking good, Golden, & Goldie had said, Go fuck yourself, Max. So Jen loves Goldie for that & for other things.

There's gonna be *cults*, Maycie moans. God, my Aunt Lydia is probably joining one as we speak. Her poor cats.

What would a cult want with your Aunt Lydia's cats? Goldie dismisses, reaching out to run a hand down The Moon's leg, entranced. The Moon lets her. Jen hasn't thought to touch The Moon, though The Moon's touched her. She wonders if The Moon's leg is smooth or just looks that way, like sharks. God, says Goldie. Look at you! You're The Moon! There's a planet in Jen's bedroom!

The moon isn't a planet, Jen says, can't help it, then glances nervously at The Moon & away. But she's right. The moon is the earth's only natural satellite, tide-bound so it always faces the earth. Kind of metaphorical if you think about it, Theia crashes into the earth, is absorbed, wrenches part of herself free, is stuck staring down at the thing that ate her body. Controls the tides but is also bound to it. Would have been a good essay. Jen regrets she didn't write it before The Moon disappeared & made essays seem small & pointless. Anyway she's called 'the' moon because she was the first one humans ever saw, didn't know others would exist. A moon, the moon, a/the. Big difference, small words. Lots to think about if you're willing to do it, something something subtext something human tendency toward narrativization of reality, inserting story where there is none. Inserting meaning there too.

Sorry, Maycie is saying on Jen's behalf, she doesn't mean anything by it. You're perfect as you are, um, cosmically speaking, I mean—

Harding holds out her hand & Maycie snaps her mouth shut, taking it & letting Harding pull her down onto the bed, head in her lap. Harding starts to idly braid her hair. Harding's own hair is pulled back into a tight, neat bun, like a stern schoolmistress from the eighteen hundreds. Her dad's big on her having long hair but she always wears it pulled up & back so you'd never know. Jen's never been over to Harding's house because there are like ten siblings & it's too overwhelming. Also they don't have air conditioning. But anyway, Jen suspects she lets her hair down there, puts it up when she leaves. When she's at college Jen bets anything she gets some sort of gay haircut. Undercut, bob. Something.

Jen lets out a long breath. Harding's calm is doing wonders for her own sense of panic. Feels like she's been given a numbing agent. She knows it's there, but it's farther away.

So, Harding says. Voice flat. Blunt. Good old Harding. You're The Moon. But this isn't the hex we did. We were trying to summon Lilith.

The Moon snorts, derisive. The 'hex' you did is a nonsensical string of Latin words some hack made up in 1940, she says. I'm not here because your stupid hex worked. I'm here because you tried to *use* me, and that's *rude*. No one even sacrifices virgins to me anymore. She sniffs like even bringing this fact up is an insult to her.

You want us to *sacrifice* a *virgin*? Maycie squeaks.

Well, that rules me out, chirps Goldie. She rolls lazily over onto her back, remarkably sanguine for a girl with the actual, literal moon in front of her. Goldie does that; she's always done it, as long as Jen's known her, slumping into a kind of droll laziness the more trouble she gets in. Ohh. Could it be a boy? Because I don't think I could kill another woman. For like, feminist reasons.

Maycie makes another little sound. Harding's hands tighten in her hair, settle her down further. She's going to disappear into the bed & Harding's lap if they're not careful, if they don't keep an eye out. What... um. What counts as being a virgin. Like does it have to be P in V or—

You're missing the point, The Moon interrupts, rolling her eyes. It was a *nice gesture*.

Not so nice for the virgin, Goldie says.

Jen frowns. But... if you don't want a virgin, and our hex

didn't do anything, why are you *here*? I mean, specifically, with *us*?

What exactly is it that you *want*, Harding clarifies. She's woven Maycie's hair into a braided crown & tied it off with a rubber band. Jen's hair is too rowdy for that sort of thing, gets frizzy & horrible & when she tries to undo it she ends up with a big rat's nest. Being a woman & having a body is a fucking nightmare. Not that Harding ever tries to play with Jen's hair. Harding's made it clear who her favorite is.

The Moon heaves a sigh, like the four of them are exhausting in their stupidity. She rolls her head to the side & examines her fingernails. I've *told* you, she says. I'm done being the moon. It's thankless work and I'm finished with it. I'm going to live here. On Earth.

But you're the moon! cries Maycie. We need you to do... do... moon stuff!

I'll do it, Goldie volunteers, clapping her hands together. I'd be sooooo cute as the moon.

Take this seriously, G, Harding scolds sharply.

Take it *seriously*? Goldie repeats, laughing. For the first time, Jen catches a slight edge of hysteria.

There you are, she thinks. Girl in the combat boots & sexy silk pajamas. I know who you are really. I've held your hair. I've heard the way you talk to your mom. I know why you're wearing your dead brother's shoes.

Goldie is saying, The fucking *moon* is in Jennifer's goddamn bedroom telling us she's, like, *bored of being the moon*, and you want me to, what, draw up a spreadsheet of possible moon replacement candidates? Should we advertise in *The*

53

Island Packet? Single Round Planet seeks replacement tidal guardian—

You can't stay on earth, Jen interrupts, before Goldie can really get going, because once she starts it's impossible to shut her up, she just goes & goes & goes. Every time you move we have an earthquake, and anyway, nobody can see you.

Yet, sings The Moon. Why do you think I came to you girls? You owe me. You're gonna help me. She smiles at the four of them the way you'd smile at a pet watching you eat. She says, I'm being nice, asking. I think Jennifer and Maycie know that I don't *have* to be nice.

Jen looks over at Harding, whose eyes have become slants as she looks back at Jen, calculating. Jen's not going to tell her about The Moon almost taking Max out. About the voice in her head saying *Easy peasy*.

Help you… stop being the moon? Jen asks.

Goldie lies back down on the floor, sprawled bonelessly on Jen's rug. Maycie is blinking with big eyes, gaze darting from Jen to The Moon to Harding & back again. Harding's phone is vibrating. *DAD*. She ignores it. Jen says: We need a moon.

And you'll have one! Just not me, The Moon promises breezily. All we need is a teeny, tiny human sacrifice. Virginity optional.

Maycie curls up into a tight ball on Harding's lap, not just her head anymore, her whole body, like she'd climb inside if she had the chance. Oh God, we are going to *prison*, she moans. Real prison. *Army* prison. We are going to get sent to *The Hague*.

The Hague isn't a prison, it's a court of law, says Jen distractedly. What is the sacrifice for?

The same thing it was always for, The Moon explains, sounding surprised. When she looks at Jen, it feels like they're back downstairs, her hand on Max's chest, his lungs pressed closed beneath them. The Moon smiles. The body, of course.

yesterday.
(jen)

They had come to Maycie's because Maycie's mom wasn't there. Harding's parents were strict and weird, Jen's parents were annoying and invasive, and Goldie's parents were having some kind of community fundraiser for something. Jen found Goldie's parents' parties incredibly off-putting. A bunch of identical women stood around in dresses of identical cuts saying nothing and steadily guzzling chardonnay while men with matching hairstyles who knew jack shit about boats gave myriad opinions on boats. Then at the end they all gave thousands of dollars to whatever whim Goldie's mother was currently endorsing and drove home drunk. So it was best to go to Maycie's, where there were no parents at all.

God if they don't kiss before everyone goes off to college it's going to be *sooo* tragic, Goldie muttered, carefully drawing the pentagram with a tube of lipstick she'd unearthed from her purse. They were up in the Winter Room, having climbed in through the window via ladder. Harding and Maycie were downstairs rounding up candles. Goldie did a little wiggle as she scooted back to give herself more room to draw; trust Goldie to make anything she did a whole performance.

Jen thought it was super obvious Harding and Maycie were, whatever, dancing around each other, but: I dunno. Maybe they're right not to. Could be dicey.

Goldie stopped her careful artwork to glare up at where Jen was sitting. She said, What do you mean, *dicey*?

Just – you know. Relationships that start in high school never work out.

Literally *today* you were all like 'Harding, tell Maycie how hot she is.'

Okay, first of all, Jen would have said *literally anything* to get them to stop talking about Jen losing her virginity to a diner line cook slash remedial math moron, or even about Jen losing her virginity at all. Jen simply felt that there was no need to talk about her virginity, at any time, ever. Virginity as a concept was a construct invented by society to arbitrarily inflate the value of selling off their daughters, so Jen didn't get why everyone was so obsessed with it, *virgin first time rough sex raw secret* etc. It was literally just advertising. Buy my daughter, she's organic. No pesticides. Sustainably raised, grass-fed. Allowed to roam between laying eggs.

I'm just saying, could be unwise, Jen said, trying not to look at the message that had popped up on Goldie's phone, from a name saved as *maximum*✏️〉. What 'maximum pen leg' meant, Jen couldn't begin to guess.

Oh my God Jen, you have *no* joie de vivre, Goldie complained, leveling Jen with the kind of look she usually reserved for waiters who tried to flirt with her. They're in *looooove*. She returned messily to work and swiped an errant streak of lipstick across her knee. Jen bent down to smudge the lipstick from Goldie's perfect tan skin. It came off on her thumb, red and sticky, so now it was Jen's problem. Typical.

maximum🖊❯ texted again. Goldie continued to ignore it.

Jen grit her teeth. Will you answer Maximum Pen Leg so he shuts up? Tell him you'll go to whatever party he's desperate to have you at and then we can all, like, move on.

Goldie blinked at her, looking with surprise at the phone clutched between her pinky and ring finger, as if she hadn't noticed it going off. Jen guessed when people texted you all the time you became inured enough to it that you didn't compulsively check to see what the messages said.

I thought you said high school parties were pathetic attempts to play at adulthood by children with no concept of what adulthood actually entails, Goldie said.

Goldie was right. Jen had said that.

Well obviously *I* don't want to go, she sniffed, and didn't add *also I am not the one being invited*. I'd like to preserve at least one brain cell before I get to college.

You know they have parties in college, right?

It's different.

How?

Because Jen was going to Yale, that was how. At Yale, parties would be with and for people like Jen. People who liked to *talk* about things, books and science and philosophy, not who hooked up with who in which broken-into tourist cabin on Daufuskie Island. Jen was above, *way* above, needing to be popular with teenagers, okay.

It just is, Jen said. Goldie wouldn't get it; Goldie *had*

hooked up in one of the broken-into tourist cabins on Daufuskie. Probably with *maximum* 🔪.

She brought to her lips the giant water bottle filled with Goldie's cocktail that they'd hauled up in a backpack. It didn't taste like anything other than juice, which could be a good or bad thing depending on whether this was because Goldie didn't put in enough vodka or if she just hid the taste with sugar and lemon. Whatever; Jen had nowhere to be. They were going to hex the moon; who cared. The cocktail was sweet in her mouth, but it finished sour. A burn in her throat.

Beside her, Goldie held out her hand for the cocktail bottle and then said, admiring her handiwork, Ahhh. Good, right?

Maycie & Harding clambered in through the window. Maycie had candles. Harding was holding a big knife from the kitchen and a teaspoon, presumably for the blood. No dibs, said Jen, nodding at it.

Not me either, said Goldie quickly. Nose game.

They touched their noses. Maycie had to drop the candles to the floor to do it.

Harding looked down at the knife. She hadn't bothered to raise a finger. Yeah, she said. I figured it'd be me.

now.

new moon minus ten hours

The Moon says, Ladies, it's not that complicated. You get me a body in the next ten hours, I take over the body, the previous occupant of the body becomes the moon, problem solved. Easy peasy.

Easy peasy, Goldie repeats dubiously.

Why ten hours, asks Jen.

Harding, Maycie, Goldie & The Moon turn to look at her. Sorry Jen is the only one thinking logically, but it's important to understand the parameters of the assignment. That's the first thing you do: you figure out the grading rubric & then you answer based on what will get you the highest score. School is not hard.

Excellent question, Jennifer, coos The Moon. Jen thinks she might actually be The Moon's favorite, which doesn't matter, obviously, Jen doesn't need The Moon's approval, but it's better to be the favorite than the least favorite regardless. The answer is because there are ten hours left of the synodic month.

The complete cycle of moon phases, Jen translates for her friends. New to new.

A-plus, Jennifer, The Moon tells her. Yes. Ten hours between now and the New Moon.

So you'll die?

I will become the New Moon.

Okay. But what's that mean. For you.

It means I become the New Moon.

You're not a very good educator, says Jen.

You're not a very good conversationalist, says The Moon.

Look, Jen says, I'm just trying to figure out what it is exactly that you need from us and why. Help me to help you.

The Moon barks out a laugh. She's not as bad as maybe Jen had thought before. Sure, she's kind of a bitch, but isn't that just what men call women with opinions? I'm Not Bossy, I'm The Boss. If I Were A Man, Then I'd Be The Man. Etc.

I don't die, The Moon tells her, turning so that she is addressing only Jen now. Jen feels a flush of pride. The Moon knows who the most useful one here is. Jen loves her friends but none of them are exactly *sensible*, maybe Harding is calm but she's still, you know, she's got all that religion stuff floating around in her head, not her fault, consequence of upbringing etc., but Jen's the one who The Moon can actually *talk* to, Jen's the *adult*.

So what happens?

Nothing, usually, says The Moon. I roll over in my sleep. Wake up new. Wake up empty. Then time passes. Humanity gives and gives and gives and I take it all in. It fills me up. It's mostly subconscious. It's given to me but it doesn't even have my name on it. Hand-me-downs. Used to be formal prayers, you know. With my hands outstretched and with a full heart, I bow to the moon. I release all that does not serve me. I release the hurt, the ignorance, and the greed, the anguish, the anger, the sorrow, the pain.

The grief, says Jen.

It's cosmic, agrees The Moon.

But you're not actually changing size, Jen points out. It's just how the light works. Part sun, part earthshine, in different ratios.

Earthshine! cries Maycie. That's so beautiful. You are my earthshine, my only earthshine, you make me happy when skies are gray.

It just means reflection, Jen tells her. The light reflected off the earth.

Please don't take my earthshine away, Maycie pouts.

It's a metaphor, Jennifer, The Moon tells her. Not everything is literal. Use your imagination.

I have a great imagination.

You have a great intellect, corrects The Moon. It's not the same thing.

Maycie reaches over & gives Jen a fortifying pat on the hand before turning to The Moon. So you've been eating all our problems and you're full.

Sick to my stomach, says The Moon. Absolutely *nauseous*.

Harding asks, Can we have a minute. To discuss our options.

You don't *have* any options, The Moon tells her. Your options are kill everybody on earth via a *spontaneous dissolution event* or get me a body. What's there to discuss?

Which body, Harding answers. She's staring down The Moon like she's not scared of her, which Jen doesn't believe for even one second.

The Moon shrugs. All right, she says. Have your privacy if you think it matters. She begins to move toward the door & the house rattles around her like she's drawing it inward. Like it wants to implode. Jen puts her hand out automatically, grabs ahold of the Instagram vase to keep it steady.

Why don't you stay here, Jen suggests. We'll go to the basement. You're going to bring the whole house down if you move too much.

Maycie hops up off of Harding's lap & grabs Goldie's hands, yanking her to her feet. Harding follows more slowly. Jen waits til they're all out of her room – hears her dad say in confusion, When did you all get here? Why'd you, what's with all this window-climbing, doesn't anybody use the door anymore – & turns to look at The Moon. They *get* each other, Jen thinks. The Moon sees the world like Jen does.

Jen says, Shit ass time to decide to come be tied to the fate of humanity.

Your perspective is limited, answers The Moon. Never a good time. Never a bad time. Only time.

Yeah but the climate. Wars. The Yellowstone Supervolcano.

There have always been wars and volcanoes, says The Moon. Little Ice Age. Big Ice Age. Dinosaurs, comets.

Jen shrugs. Whatever; if The Moon wants to die in the water wars that's her business. Okay. But why now. I mean why with only ten hours left. Seems like a big risk.

I have found that humanity operates most efficiently under acute time pressure, says The Moon, like she knows everything. But maybe it's one of those things. She doesn't spin, after all. Can't turn away. Has to see it all, all the time, no blinking, no eyes falling shut. Part sun, part earthshine. But it's all light, really, in the end. The only difference is its potency.

Jennifer, says The Moon, leaning in, her voice gone layered again, & this time Jen thinks they sound familiar, the voices, but she can't place why. You're not like your mother, are you?

Jen stiffens. What's that supposed to mean?

The Moon shrugs. She reaches out & runs her finger along the edge of Jen's cheek; it's cold. She says, You're clever. Figure it out.

Jen leaves The Moon & follows her friends downstairs & then downstairs again, to the basement. They're one of the few houses on the island to have one. Whenever the weather's bad enough the whole neighborhood comes & waits out the storm. Just in case. Most people don't evacuate, even when they're supposed to. Nobody ever thinks they're going to die. *Acute time pressure*, ha. The Moon's right.

So obviously we're not going to *murder* anyone, Maycie says as soon as Jen arrives. She glances around at them. I mean. Right?

Goldie stretches herself out on the carpet. Her pajama top rolls up, exposing her stomach. She says, Of course not.

Jen looks at Harding. Harding looks at Jen. Jen thinks: You're not like your mother, are you?

Not if there's another option, Harding agrees, but she's holding Jen's gaze, & Jen knows that what she's thinking is that they're the grown-ups, & if there isn't another way... well. If there's a lesson to be learned from Jen's mess of a mother it's surely that there's no point in getting overly emotional, & Jen's not. Jen's *not*.

If, repeats Goldie. Fuck all the way off, you couldn't murder somebody. God would be too mad.

Harding shakes her head with a sigh. God's already mad at me, she says, which makes no sense because as far as Jen can see Harding never does anything wrong, ever.

Jen offers, Utilitarian philosophy says—

Shut up about philosophy Jen, this is real fucking life, snaps Goldie. You're telling me you could kill someone? Like really kill them?

Easy peasy, The Moon had said, her hand on Max's chest. But that wasn't Jen doing it. Jen had stopped her. *Your perspective is limited.* She'd told Jen to be reasonable. Jen *is* reasonable, Jen is above being emotional about things, but. But. She shivers.

No, Jen admits. I mean, I don't know. Obviously I don't want to. I'm just saying we have to be prepared for all eventualities.

That's a really psychotic thing to say, Goldie tells her. Like, chilling. It's insane we're even talking about this.

That's one of the options she gave us, but there must be others, Harding says, reasonably in Jen's opinion. We just have to think of them.

Goldie folds her arms across her chest. It's not a fucking *option*, she says. We're not going to kill anybody. *I'm* not.

What if, Maycie pipes up timidly, what if we just. Hex her back? That's what got her here, right?

She said it wasn't the hex itself, Jen reminds her.

65

Maybe she lied, says Maycie. I mean. We're just blindly trusting that she's telling us the truth, right? But we did a hex and now she's here. So.

Jen looks at Harding, who shrugs. Worth a shot. She flexes her hand where she'd sliced it yesterday; wouldn't be hard to reopen. Goldie is already on her phone, thumbs skittering. They gather around her, peering over her shoulder. She's typed *reverse hex*. First result, geeksforgeeks.org:

Efficient approach: The idea is to use shift operators only.

Move the position of the last byte to the first byte using left shift operator(<<).

Move the position of the first byte to the last byte using right shift operator(>>).

Move the middle bytes using the combination of left shift and right shift operator.

Apply logical OR (|) to the output of all the above expression, to get the desired output.

Well that's useless, says Maycie. Is that like a coding thing?

Goldie shrugs, types *how to reverse a hex*, & hits enter. Now we're cooking, she says, & scrolls to the second result, spells8.com:

Reversing a Hex with Mirror. Learn to create a spiritual barrier to protect you against psychic attacks. This post includes three ways to send a curse back to its originator.

No good, Harding says, reading over Goldie's shoulder. We *are* the originators.

Third result, wikiHow.com:

NATURE & PAGAN BELIEFS >> WICCA
How to Reverse a Curse

You might suspect you're cursed if you've been having nightmares, seeing omens, and dealing with illness or bad luck. Feeling cursed can be scary, but you may be able to protect yourself. Taking a salt bath or smudging yourself may cleanse away any negative energy directed toward you including a minor curse.

Take a salt bath, Jen repeats incredulously. A *salt* bath.

Get what you pay for, Goldie returns. Free website says take a salt bath. 1 cup salt, quarter-cup baking soda—

Why *baking soda*?

I don't fucking *know*, Jen, I'm just reading what the website says. Salt, baking soda, essential oil if you have it—

We don't.

Okay, fine then, no essential oil. Poor man's salt bath, whatever. It says we need to visualize positive energy flowing into the bath in the form of a solid beam of light while soaking for at least thirty to forty minutes and reciting this prayer… spell… thing.

Beat of quiet. It's so stupid. Jen looks around at three dubious faces. Everyone clearly thinks it's as stupid as she does, but on the other hand, their other immediate option seems to be murder, so. Maybe Jen will take stupid as a first swing. Nothing wrong with a bad first swing, & who knows, this whole thing is already so insane, maybe it'll work. It had seemed stupid when they were doing the hex the first time; a stupid idea's not stupid if it works.

I should do it, Harding decides. Take the bath, I mean. Since I'm the one who cut my hand. It's my blood, right? So it should probably be me.

Maybe we should all take the bath, says Maycie. It was your blood but we were all there.

We're not all going to fit in my bath unless we hang our legs off the side, Jen tells her regretfully, but to her surprise this does not seem to shake Maycie's resolve. She just shrugs.

Okay, so we hang our legs off the side, she says. Nowhere in the wikiHow article does it say you have to be, like, fully submerged.

This is so fucking dumb, Jen states, out loud, just so someone has, & to be the one who did. But Goldie is already off the floor & stomping up the stairs. Maycie & Harding follow up after. Jen trails behind, the only one who knows where the cooking stuff is, so she sends the three of them up to run the bath & goes into the kitchen.

Her dad's sitting at the kitchen table, staring down at his phone. Calls still not going through, Jen guesses. She grabs the saltshaker & the box of baking soda. Her dad looks up briefly, raises an eyebrow, looks back down again. Clearly isn't going to ask. Unsurprising: her dad is very self-oriented. That's a word Jen learned when her mom made them all go to family therapy. She also learned the phrase *utility monster*, which the therapist had said meant someone who thought that getting their way gave them greater utility than the people whose desires were sidelined in the sacrifice. The therapist had asked Jen whether she thought anyone she knew might be defined that way. Jen had said, No, why?

Upstairs in the bathroom, Goldie, Harding, & Maycie are sitting naked in the bath as the water runs over them, slowly filling up. Harding's in the middle. Goldie's under the faucet.

This looks like the start of like, a *very* weird porn, Jen tells them dubiously. Why are you guys naked.

We realized if we got our underwear wet then we'd have to all borrow your underwear, Maycie explains, and that felt weirder than being naked.

I have *bathing suits*.

Yeah but they're in your room, right? And The Moon's in there.

You can leave your underwear on, Harding offers, like she's doing Jen a favor. Since you have dry clothes to change into.

Jen strips. Her friends are naked, she's not going to be the embarrassed teenager not willing to get her tits out just because she's not The Hot One. Jen gets in beside Maycie, shoves them all over a little. Maycie slides a little bit onto Harding's leg; Goldie yelps as the faucet digs into her shoulder. Jen releases the salt & the baking soda & watches it spread in the water around them.

They sit quietly for a minute.

What was the prayer, Harding asks, & Goldie says, Oh right! & reaches for where her phone is balanced precariously on the ledge. She pulls up the wikiHow article & reads out, Salt and water make me pure, bring me now the perfect cure, let this water make me free, as I will so mote it be.

Oh my God it rhymes, Jen mutters. This is so—

Salt and water make me pure, Harding cuts in, her voice low & serious. Bring me now the perfect cure, let this water make me free, as I will so mote it be. Salt and water make me pure, bring me now the perfect cure, let this water make me free, as I will so mote it be.

Jen falls quiet as Harding recites it, over & over. It's dumb but it becomes a sort of singsong, low & soothing, Harding's scratchy voice making Jen's eyes flutter a little. Maycie joins in quietly, then Goldie. Jen resists. Jen thinks it's stupid. Jen's not going to lose her head just because—

Maycie shoves her elbow into Jen's side & Jen squeaks out: Salt and water make me pure, bring me now the perfect cure, let this water make me free, as I will so mote it be.

The house shakes.

The door slams open.

They stop chanting.

The Moon says, Stop embarrassing yourselves, get the fuck out of the bath.

goldie

now.

new moon minus nine hours

Goldie is named after half an old Jamaican dancehall song by Tenor Saw, born Clive Bright. 'Golden Hen'. '*Well, I've been searching from morning, morning / For my golden hen / Because she's my best friend*'. Henry was the other half. Golden & Henry, Goldie & Hen, Golden Hen. Henry is dead. Has been for ages. Four years. August 8, 2019. Got on a boat, did drugs, died. Loads of people would, right after, so everybody made a huge deal about it and then immediately forgot. Lockdown did Goldie good, didn't have to be in school with everyone looking at her, poor girl dead brother. Weird sense of self-righteousness at the pandemic, everyone else dying too: see how you like it. Now we all have dead relatives, ha.

Goldie's the only one of them who's ever been to the morgue, which is probably why Goldie's the one to think of it, back in her clothes and hunched miserably on Jen's bed while The Moon dresses them all down for trying to find an alternative solution to their problem.

How fresh does it have to be? Goldie asks. The body.

I'm too beautiful to get into a mummy, The Moon says.

I don't think they mummify people anymore, says Maycie. Not even, you know, in Egypt.

That's racist, Maycie, Goldie says.

Maycie frowns. I don't think it's racist to *mention* Egypt.

Yeah but to say they mummify people.

But they famously *did* mummify people.

Yeah but—

Guys, interjects Harding. Enough. Goldie and Maycie fall silent. Harding's just got that kind of power, she says *do this* and people go ahead and do it. If girls were allowed to be priests in her denomination she'd be pope for sure.

Could you, like, Goldie resumes, refocusing, reanimate a body? If it's new enough. Like *fresh* off the runway.

The Moon considers Goldie. It's unnerving when she looks at you. It's like she's looking at you and inside of you and through you all at once. She's been thinking things into Goldie's head all night: *Nice shorts* and *Max certainly likes them* and *Give him a twirl, my Golden Hen.* And Jen's clearly like, in love with The Moon or whatever because Jen pretends she's above it all but she's actually pathetic for anyone who shows her even a spot of attention. This is why Goldie wants her to fuck Six-Pack before she goes off to college, because otherwise she'll be a sitting duck for some asshole at Yale who sees easy pickings and ruins her life.

The Moon says, Depends.

Great, says Goldie, clapping her hands onto her knees and standing. Then it's decided.

What's decided? Maycie asks.

Jen is frowning at her. Jen hates it when people other than Jen have good ideas. But Harding is looking at Goldie with interest and patience and it gives her confidence, sort of, so she straightens up her shoulders. We're going to go to the morgue.

Oh, mutters Jen, grudgingly impressed. That's smart.

Yes, well, some of us get creative when our options are limited, Goldie tells her.

How do we get into the morgue? Maycie asks, a little fretful, but nevertheless getting to her feet and slipping her shoes on. Maycie's a trooper. Goldie's always liked that about her. She tries everything once, even the stuff that's unappealing. You have to admire that in a person, Goldie's always thought so.

I don't think anybody's going to be paying particularly close attention to who's going in and out right now, Jen tells her dryly. Bigger concerns. Moon out of the sky etcetera.

What about The Moon? Harding asks, turning to look at her. Every time she moves we have an earthquake.

Oh, I was just doing that for fun, The Moon says. I can turn it off.

All three of them turn to look at her. Jen says: Are you fucking for real. The Moon smiles at them, serene, and lifts one shoulder in an elegant shrug. Then why did you break all my mom's nice shit!

Not all of it, The Moon says, nodding at this horrifically ugly vase that Jen's been neurotically protective of all night. Don't you ever do things just because you want to? Just because it feels good?

No, says Jen. I'm civilized.

The Moon laughs. Oh, Jennifer, she coos, mocking. Then she claps her hands together, loud enough that from downstairs Goldie hears WHAT THE FUCK WAS THAT? from Max. The Moon smirks, unapologetic. Oops. Out of practice. Shall we?

Harding looks over at Jen. Your dad, she says.

Shit, mutters Jen. She goes to lock the door. If he yells in and I don't answer he'll know something's up. But.

But at least we'll have a head start, says The Moon, and as she does, the layered voices filter out until there's only one left. She sounds like Jen. She sounds *exactly* like Jen. Goldie shivers.

Freaky, says Maycie.

It's perfect, says Goldie. You stay here and be Jen. We'll go get you a body.

What if her dad wants to come into the room? Harding points out. The voice is good, but he'll know it's not her if the room is empty.

He won't come in if I tell him not to, Jen says. He believes in personal autonomy for children.

Harding stares at her. What does that mean.

Goldie forgets, sometimes. That Harding's parents are so weird. That there's no locks on any of the doors in their house except the bathroom.

Yeah, it's a policy, Jen goes on, oblivious to Harding's incredulity. My space is mine. Max's space is Max's. Their space is theirs. It's like a whole thing.

Great, then it's settled. The Moon is Jen. Out the window, ladies, Goldie says, and jumps first.

yesterday.
(harding)

Harding and Maycie were trying to find Maycie's mom's candles. There were tons lying around, but most of them were colorful and scented and Goldie insisted they use white candles, no smell. You couldn't do a hex in a room that smelled like Summer Breeze apparently. Harding turned from where she was looking in a low cupboard in the mud room; when she did, Maycie was there, very close.

Hi, Harding said.

Tell me I'm hot, demanded Maycie, inserting herself so completely into Harding's space that it made her dizzy. Harding was always trying to stop, to have each time be the last time. But every time Maycie wrinkled her nose and put her body next to Harding's, all her resolve whited out into an endless, frictionless ramp of desire that she had no recourse but to slip down until something braced her fall.

Why? Harding asked, even as Maycie got closer, pouting her lips.

I want you to.

Why? asked Harding again.

Maycie huffed, impatient. I just *do*.

Harding sighed. She reached out and grabbed the pocket

of Maycie's shorts, dragged her in further. Maycie squeaked a little, fell forward without grace. Harding nudged their noses together. Maycie's skin was smooth, and warm. Maycie was always so warm. The pout fell off Maycie's face and she went still. Maycie always did this, too. Teased Harding into playing the game, and then panicked when Harding took her turn.

Maycie danced away, out of Harding's grip, and laughed, light and false. Ah, ha! I knew it. I knew you thought I was hot. Embarrassing for you. She looked away and into a cupboard, rummaging around. When Maycie wasn't in the room Harding had such logical plans, made such reasonable decisions. It would be easier when she went. When Harding was at Liberty and Maycie was in Argentina, of all places. Then Harding would be able to just… think.

Harding gently pulled Maycie's hand from the cupboard door. Tugged her back a few steps. Maycie came to her, easy. She stared at Harding's shoulder so Harding ducked her head. Her face felt like it was on fire, her mouth sticky, gumming up. Harding had never been good at saying things but now she said: I think you're hot. She pressed their mouths together and Maycie let her, opened up beautifully, relaxed. Harding wrapped her arms around Maycie's waist and Maycie's arms came around Harding's neck. Her mouth was warm and her skin was warm and Harding wanted to stop feeling like this. She wanted. She.

Harding drew back. She shivered.

Maycie's eyes opened and she giggled. Be normal, she demanded, light again, teasing again. Having gotten what she wanted.

I want to bite you I want to glue our hands together I want to explode I want to explode, Harding didn't say, because that was Harding's problem, she was too intense, she was always too intense. Her dad was always saying it. Everyone was always saying it.

Maycie laughed. Light and easy. Maycie made everything look so easy. Harding wondered what it was like. Maycie had no parental supervision at all. Maycie could do whatever she liked, and often did. She talked to her mother the way you might talk to a kid you were babysitting. Once Harding had heard her mother say *Maycie my darling please be careful around the firepit* and Maycie had said back *God will you give it a rest Maureen*, and instead of grounding Maycie for the rest of her natural life Maycie's mother had said *All right, all right, sorry.*

If Harding said *God will you give it a rest* to her mother she'd never see outside of the house again.

Aha! Maycie cried, straightening up. I found them! I *knew* they kept some in here. Her hands were full of candles.

Good job, Maceface, Harding said. Now I'll go get the knife.

Knife? Maycie repeated. Why do we need a knife?

Harding shrugged. That's how these things work, she said. *Someone* always has to bleed.

now.
new moon minus eight hours

As it turns out, when the moon disappears from the sky people stop paying attention to who comes in and out of the hospital. Fab. Everyone in the ER's staring up at the TV, which is playing C-SPAN. They're talking about the moon being gone, duh. The ticker along the bottom assures the watcher that President Biden is working closely with NASA to understand the full scope of the situation.

The Moon's a bitch, actually, Goldie says to the nurse behind the counter as they pass her by, and she barely even tears her eyes from the screen as she mumbles, Huh?

Nobody stops them from going through the doors down the hall, or getting in the elevator and going down to the basement. Nobody's even in the hallway. The morgue's locked, not really a surprise, she guesses it's because of how awful people are. She's seen all that stuff online, on TikTok and stuff, about how hospitals prefer to hire women in morgues, because men are more likely to fuck the cadavers. Anne Boleyn's ladies-in-waiting cleaned her head and body themselves because they were afraid someone would try to fuck it. Richard Poncher had himself buried face down on top of Marilyn Monroe. She bets there are other examples; those are just the ones she knows. Anyway, now she knocks on the door. Guy (!) comes out. Can I help you?

Did you hear about the moon? Goldie asks, making her eyes wide.

Guy blinks. Uh. What?

The. *Moon*, says Goldie again, gesturing at her friends, who nod like *yeah man, the moon*. It disappeared.

He laughs, sort of, like he's confused, like this is a bad joke. Goldie *knew* they wouldn't have thought to tell him down here. Nobody likes to come down. When they'd had to identify Henry she hadn't seen anyone at all and the nurse had sort of shuffled awkwardly behind them, waiting.

Goldie shoves her phone under the guy's nose. I'm not joking, it's just like, *gone*, she tells him. The lady at the desk sent us down to tell you about it. She said she didn't think anyone had told you, and the cell service is bad down here.

Who did? Emily?

Oh, Emily, totally, that's it I think. Right Jen?

Yeah, says Jen. Emily for sure.

Harding's gone round Goldie's shoulder and is pretending to look at Goldie's phone but her foot is right in front of the door. Anyway, now we've told you, Goldie says. Guess we should go, my friend's got PMS.

Wait, wait. I don't understand what you're saying. You think your friend's PMS has something to do with the moon?

Dude, that's an *insane* thing to say, Goldie scoffs. Look, just go talk to Emily, okay? She'll explain everything. We're all freaking out up there. C'mon, it's creepy down here I don't wanna stay with all these dead bodies, blech. She walks back toward the door, Jen and Maycie at her sides, Harding staying behind. Foot in the door. Guy comes with them, sort of dazed. People are all so predictable, men in particular, Goldie is barely even trying. She just sort of blathers on at him as he gets on the elevator, rides it back up. Points at Emily, who looks up and says Oh God Jared did you *see*.

They turn back round. Get into the elevator. Downstairs. Harding, foot in the door. Goldie thinks about The Moon in her head saying *easy peasy*.

Inside the morgue it's cold as shit, they always are, to keep the bodies from rotting. Not all the bodies get embalmed. They cremated Henry, for example. The ashes were sort of… clumpy. Movies made it look different than it was, more ethereal. When Goldie had dumped them out she'd seen a tooth hit the ground, roll away.

What do we do now? Maycie asks, timid as always.

Goldie loops an arm around her shoulders, bops their heads together gently. Pick a body, any body, she says, and gestures expansively with her other hand. We should probably try to find a good one, like, one that's pretty and not all fucked up. The Moon seems like a no uggos kind of bitch.

It's a dead body, Goldie, I don't think we're going to find any cover girls, Jen says flatly, in her typical Jen way. Excuse Goldie for trying to make the best of a bad situation.

Harding's already opening up the slabs and poking her head in. Outstanding. She's unflappable. Old, she says by way of explanation as she pulls her head back out, closes the door. Opens another. Also old.

Mine's old too. How're there so many old people on this island if they're all dead in this morgue, Jen grumbles.

Young! cries Maycie, and then, Oh.

What?

Really, um. She closes the door quickly, puts a hand over her mouth. Not in good shape below the shoulders. Oh God.

Harding goes over, puts a hand on Maycie's back. Sweet. Goldie nudges Jen, nods toward them. Waggles her eyebrows. Jen rolls her eyes. No fun, ever.

Got one! cries Jen triumphantly, throwing the slab door further open and then pulling the body out into the open. It's a youngish woman, probably in her early thirties if Goldie had to guess. Pretty enough, nothing super obviously wrong.

What'd she die of? Harding asks, curling her body around Maycie so Maycie doesn't have to look. Maycie peeks around her anyway. Trooper, Goldie thinks again, fondly.

Jen flicks the body's tag around. Ummm. Says heart attack brought on by… oh. She glances nervously at Goldie, and that's all she needs to know. Henry in the water. Face down. Everyone's still so weird about it, but that was Henry for you, full speed always, a sweet idiot. People die for all kinds of reasons, none better than the other, no point to any of it, that's just how it works. She forces her voice to sound droll and bored. OD? she guesses. That's not too bad then, she'll have slept off the detox period, as it were.

Slept off, Maycie mutters.

How are we going to get it out of here? Harding wonders, always practical.

There's a back exit, Goldie tells her. When you come to identify a body they send you out a different way so you don't have to, like, see people.

Her friends look at her silently. She'd been the one to identify Henry. Her mom couldn't bear it. Her dad couldn't tell. Henry was too bloated and purple, and he'd been in the water so long a gator had chomped off a piece of his face, taken a chunk of his stomach. They'd sewed him up but even if they hadn't, Goldie would have recognized him. He was the other half of all her sentences. Well, I've been searching from morning, morning / For my golden hen. *Found you*, she'd said, quietly, and the nurse with her had said *I'm Sorry For Your Loss*.

We should put some clothes on her, Jen says, after clearing her throat.

Mm, Harding agrees, and shrugs off her shirt, handing it to Jen to dress the body with. She's wearing a sports bra underneath, so it almost looks like a regular outfit, if you were anyone other than Harding.

The shirt's long enough to work as a dress if you were a real slut about it, but Goldie feels bad about making the body go commando. She casts around but there isn't anywhere obvious that they might store the clothing people came in wearing. She sighs and tugs down her shorts.

Uh, Jen says. What are you doing?

We can't drag her around with her cooch out, Goldie says crossly. I'm giving her my underwear.

All three of the other girls make varying faces of surprise and distaste. Goldie huffs. Look, I'm not hyped about it either, but as a feminist I feel like I can't in good conscience shine this woman's pussy spotlight on the entire island.

Don't say pussy spotlight, Jen scolds immediately, her neck

going red. Jen's a prude. Goldie ignores her other than to roll her eyes. She pulls her pajama shorts back up and then tosses her underwear at Jen, who screams and steps back. They land squarely on the dead woman's face.

Fuck's sake, Jen, Goldie sighs.

You startled me! Jen protests. You can't just... those are your—

Harding steps forward and, without fanfare, grabs the underwear and shimmies them up the dead girl's legs. There, she says, satisfied. Two of you get her arms. Maycie and me'll get her feet.

She's heavier than she looks, but that's dead bodies for you. With significant struggle and a couple of near misses when Jen steps on her long hair and nearly sends them all sprawling, they manage to get her out to the parking lot and into Goldie's car, though by the time they get her settled there are dirt stains all over the back of Harding's shirt. Whatever. Once The Moon's reanimated her she can pick through Jen's closet for something clean that she likes.

I wonder what her name was, Maycie murmurs. Jen, did it say on the tag?

Jen shakes her head. Jane Doe, I guess.

Hello, Jane, says Maycie, soft. Sorry about this. But if you think about it, we're maybe sort of doing you a favor, you know? This is a second chance. You get to be the moon!

Stop talking to it, Goldie commands. It's not a person.

Yes, *she* is, Maycie replies, scowling. And you think so too or you wouldn't have given her your underwear.

Goldie shifts, discomfort prickling the back of her neck.

Maycie doesn't know shit. Goldie had sacrificed her underwear not for Jane Doe herself but for, you know, the spirit of the thing.

She's a dead junkie, Goldie says flatly, and doesn't flinch.

Goldie, Harding scolds.

What? Goldie snaps back. I'm right. If she were alive you wouldn't spend one second trying to get to know her because she'd probably be blitzed out of her mind freaking everybody out.

Henry hadn't been like that. Not usually. Goldie hadn't even known what was wrong until it was too late – he was too good at hiding it, too quicksilver with his jokes and his disappearances, always laughing and dragging Goldie along on his various adventures. He'd always been looking for the next thing, the next excitement, the next risk, always, since the day they came into the world one right after the other, holding hands. Of course he'd tried drugs. Of course he'd loved them. Of course he'd thrown everything away chasing more.

Once he'd come into Goldie's room, eyes strange, and swung her around, laughing manically. He'd said *G, do you see it?* and she'd asked *See what?* and Henry had covered her face with kisses and sighed dreamily. *The whole world.*

Existential issue, Jen says now, joking badly. As a general rule, poor Jen isn't very funny, or at least not when she's trying to be. She never gets the tone quite right. Look, it doesn't matter. We get her back to my house, put The Moon in her, and call it a day.

They ride the rest of the way to Jen's house in a kind of anticipatory silence; Goldie spares the thought that Henry

86

would love it actually, the disappearance, the hole in the sky. Henry would want to see what happened with the tides. Henry would love the threat of doom curling around every corner of the island, every corner of the world.

We're not gonna be able to get her up and through the window without roughing her up pretty badly, Harding muses as they pull into the driveway. Jen's dad can be seen through the kitchen window, on the phone – maybe he's finally gotten through to Jen's mother.

We can use the back door. But we'll have to pass by Max's room, so Goldie or Maycie is gonna have to distract him. He thinks you guys are the hot ones, Jen says, as if breaking bad news. No offense, Harding.

None taken, says Harding, bone-dry.

Maycie looks at Goldie. Goldie looks at Maycie.

Goldie sighs. The Moon in her head. *Give him a twirl, my Golden Hen.* She gets that feeling again, like everything is closing in on her, like everyone is standing too close, their sweat smearing her skin.

Fucking *fine*, she mutters, and in her head The Moon begins laughing, high and bright as the flickering stars.

yesterday.
(maycie)

Maycie and Goldie were the first to become friends. Before Maycie's parents' divorce turned her mom into a big embarrassing free love hippie, they'd been frequent attendees at Goldie's parents' parties. Goldie had always been beautiful, even when she was just a kid. She had the kind of face you expected to see in movies, on magazine covers.

Henry had been, too, delicate and bright. Maycie was the only one of them who'd really known Henry at all, and known him before his quick slip into the strange half-person he'd become by the end. Maycie hadn't known it was drugs; she hadn't even known people their age could *get* drugs. But even then, even when his gaze was always dreamy and far-away, he'd always been kind to Maycie. To everybody. Lovely and unearthly and kind.

Maycie didn't think she would ever forget what he had looked like, body rucked up into the oyster bed. Maycie had left the house because her parents were screaming at one another. She'd taken herself out on a walk with the dog – Doug, her father's, gone with him now to Savannah – and she'd seen a shape in the soft spotlight of the moon. Doug had started barking and pulled her toward it. She'd gone, curious, and there he was.

Pale. So bloated it made his too-thin skin look like it was struggling to contain him. His eyes had been open. Maycie had known it was him immediately, had recognized his clothes even if his distorted face was nearly unrecognizable, his favorite leather combat boots.

Henry, she had said, voice tremulous. She knew he wouldn't answer but she thought she had to try anyway. *Henry?*

He'd floated, silent. Staring up at the sky. Maycie had crawled down the retaining wall even though the oyster shells cut at her feet at the bottom, reaching out a tremulous hand to shake him. He was cold, and oddly squishy, and Maycie felt bile in her throat. Henry, she'd said again, and then noticed how his boots were cutting into his skin, and with hands that acted of their own accord she quickly unlaced them, pulling them off, as if it would help, as if this were all owing to cut circulation at his ankles. She tossed the boots up toward the road and then took another inch toward him. But as she reached forward again, Doug began frantically snarling and from the water the gator came, mouth open. Its teeth closed around Henry's side and dragged him down deeper into the water, red spreading out around him, expression unchanging.

Maycie had scrambled over the oysters and sprinted back toward the house, Doug at her heels, blood scored into her hands from the ragged shells. She wanted to scream, but when she reached the front door the sound died in her throat, leaving her hollow. She felt empty of everything except horror, replaying how Henry's dead hand had bobbed on the water's surface as the gator struggled to pull him under.

Her parents turned from where they were standing in the kitchen, hurling insults at each other. Maycie's mother said, *You're pale as the moon. Good God, what happened to your hands?*

And Maycie had said, *I fell, that's all,* and gone to bed, shaking. She had thrown up in her bathroom and climbed under her bedcovers and closed her eyes, unsure why she didn't say anything, unsure why she didn't scream, but the thought of telling her parents what she had seen – the thought of becoming little more to Goldie than the one who saw Henry eaten by the gator and did nothing to help him – stopped her tongue. She couldn't say a word for days and days and days not even when they found him and identified him, not even when Goldie, weeping and thin, had clutched at Maycie's arm and trembled through the funeral, not even when her parents sat her down and said *We Love You Just As We Always Have But We've Decided—*

Maycie, Jen said, snapping her fingers in front of Maycie's face. Focus up.

Maycie blinked, looking down at where Goldie had drawn the pentagram and set all the candles. They were holding hands around it. Maycie realized she was supposed to be saying something. Sorry, she said, looking nervously about her. Sorry, I... I was thinking.

About? Goldie prompted, droll as ever. Most of the time, Maycie managed to forget about Henry. About this thing that she knew and nobody else did. But something about the night, the Winter Room, the five of them around the pentagram...

Maycie felt something inside her trembling, calling out, being beckoned. Like the secret wanted to rise to the surface, sure and determined as the tide. It wanted to come out. Her mouth wanted to say it, her hands wanted to let go of Harding's and Jen's and cup around her lips so she could scream that it was Maycie who had taken off Henry's boots and tossed them onto the road, Maycie who had steered Goldie surreptitiously in that direction on their walk so she could find them and pull them on, not noticing the spot of blood on the heels that Maycie knew was her own. But now it rose up in her like it wanted to be said, like it wanted her to release it, all the hurt, the ignorance, and the greed, the anguish, the anger, the sorrow, the pain.

I don't know about this, Maycie choked out, staring at Goldie's feet, clad as always in poor dead Henry's boots. What do we want to hex that fat old lady for anyway? Let's go back downstairs.

But Harding took her hand back, held it tight. Her expression was set and determined, the way it got sometimes when she looked at Maycie, when it was just the two of them. No, she said. I want to do it.

But *why*?

I just do, Harding said, turning now to look at her, expression fierce, an echo of Maycie's own words. And Maycie couldn't say anything else because it was three against one, because Harding always caved when *Maycie* asked, because she didn't even fully believe it herself, that it was real, that it would do anything. She swallowed her secrets back down. She forced a laugh and said, Fine, but if the moon falls from the sky and crushes us I'm going to be so fucking mad.

now.

new moon minus seven hours

Jen, Maycie, and Harding shuffle the body in through the door while Goldie holds it open and then shakes her hair out. They wait, wincing from the weight of Jane Doe, and Goldie goes ahead to knock on Max's door once they're hidden around the corner. He opens it and stares at her for a second. Uh, he says. What?

Hello Maximum, she says. I just wondered if you'd, like, read anything new on what's going on. Can I come in?

Max hesitates for a second, then narrows his eyes, craning his head into the hallway and looking around. Where's Jen?

Upstairs.

She's got a computer too.

Yeah but she keeps giving me commentary, Goldie says, rolling her eyes, conspiratorial. Boys love it when they feel like you're in cahoots with them, like you have a shared secret. I just want the *facts*, you know?

Oh, uh, okay, Max mutters, neck going a little red, and if Jen hadn't told Goldie all the shit she'd seen on his computer Goldie might even think he was sort of sweet for it. She pushes into his room and feels his eyes on her the same way she could always feel them. She keeps her expression schooled. Well, um.

Reddit says NASA is going to try to send up a rocket.

Wow, says Goldie. Behind Max, the door still open, her friends are slowly and laboriously shuffling down the hallway, body dragging between them. Goldie shifts her shoulder a little, lets the strap of her shirt fall, watches Max's eyes follow the movement.

If she's honest, Goldie doesn't mind being the one here. Max is cute, in his own way. She's always thought so, but lately more than ever, going to his bar and being let in because she knows him, getting served beer because she knows him, following him into the alley out back and letting him fuck her up against the wall because she knows him and there's something sharp and sweet about it, that he's Jen's and Jen hates him and Jen thinks she's so much better and more mature than Goldie but Goldie knows more about life than Jen does, than Jen probably ever will.

Goldie thinks it's sort of funny that he's such a pervert. Or… well. What she thinks is funny is that Jen's so freaked out about it, like all men don't watch porn, don't watch videos with names like 'Stepdad shows daughter how to take it' and jerk off on their twin beds and then go eat dinner without washing their hands.

There's something about it that Goldie even sort of, well, it's hard to explain but there's something about how gross they all are that she *likes*. She likes what dumb animals they can be. She can make them feel good or she can make them feel like nothing and that feels good. It feels *powerful*.

Nice pajamas, Max says, and light spills down onto his shoulders. Goldie looks up and there she is, The Moon, perched on the top of his dresser, beaming. *My Golden Hen*, she laughs into Goldie's head, winkingly, knowingly. Getting it, Goldie thinks. Jen thinks Goldie's this big dumb slut but The Moon knows what Goldie knows, which is that Henry had always been chasing the next excitement, the next risk, but they had come into the world one right after the other, holding hands. Goldie was always chasing something too.

Thanks, Goldie says, and feels giddy with it, with the warm approval of The Moon above her, with the hungry look on Max's face. She cocks her head to the side and hitches herself up onto his desk. We could all die tonight.

Max takes a step closer. Yeah?

Yeah. If you think about it. Spontaneous dissolution event.

Max reaches out. His hand is shaking a little. Goldie hadn't planned to have sex with him, here, in Jen's house, Jen just upstairs, but suddenly she wants to. The whole night has already been such a clusterfuck, and she's felt helpless and flailing and small, and it feels good to instead be in control here, in this room, warm in moonlight only she can see. Max's jittery fingers are sliding up her thigh, to the mouth of her tiny shorts, further beneath the lip, further, and then hissing in surprise when he touches her. No underwear. She's given it to Jane Doe.

Goldie grins, widens her legs, lets him step into them, door still open, who cares now, her friends are gone and so's the body, Goldie's having an awful night and it feels *good*, Max's hand on her, Max pushing up into the vee of her thighs, breath coming harshly as he buries his face into the curve of her neck, says, Fuuuuck. You're always so… Jesus, you're not even wearing any—

C'mon, Maxie, she coos, rocking slightly upward, and it feels good, it feels good, his hand is big as it slips forward, slips in, touches something inside of her that always makes her gasp, his mouth latching onto her shoulder over the strap of her pajama shirt, hot and wet. *Easy peasy.*

GOLDIE, Jen's voice echoes from up the stairs, signaling that they've managed to get where they needed to be. WHERE'D YOU GO?

Max goes still.

Goldie laughs. Wriggles away, hops down, leaves him leaning against the desk with extremely tense shoulders. It almost feels better than having sex would have, watching how miserable he is as he looks back at her, mouth agape, like he can't believe that they'd started or that they'd stopped.

Poor Maximum Penny, she says, maybe next time! and blows him a kiss before leaving him there, his big embarrassing boner making his sweatpants hang awkwardly on him.

Golden! Max shouts after her. What the fuck!

Goldie laughs again, giddy with it now, restored almost, this was what Henry had been chasing too, poor Henry taking drugs so he could see the entire world when Goldie had learned how to do it just by an act of will and an act of desire, when Goldie could hold an entire person in the palm of her hand.

She darts up the stairs and waves at Jen, worries washed away, so easy. So easy. The Moon in her mind, laughing, saying *Golden after all*, pleased, and when Jen gives her a look of suspicion Goldie waves it off. Jen doesn't have to know. Not her business. Jen wouldn't get it, always gets weird about sex

95

and boys, doesn't know how to fit it into her conception of self. Not Goldie's fault.

In Jen's bedroom, Jane Doe is laid out on the bed, and The Moon is settled on the windowsill, glittering with delight as Goldie comes inside. Hello, Golden, she drawls. Having fun playing with your food? No wonder you're always so hungry.

Goldie shouts a laugh, ignoring Maycie's alarmed look. The Moon gets it, she thinks, The Moon isn't such a bitch after all. Jen wouldn't get it and Maycie wouldn't get it and *Harding* certainly wouldn't get it but The Moon does. Goldie had misjudged her. So? What do we do now? Do you just hop on inside, or…?

The Moon stands. Goldie braces for the shake but it doesn't come, the house stays stable and still. She walks over to the body and runs her hands along it, slow, thoughtful.

You thought nobody saw you in the moonlight, touching dead things, The Moon murmurs. But I *am* the moonlight, and I did. I always do. Always.

Goldie glances at Jen, eyebrows rising. Jen shrugs, but beside her Maycie's eyes are wide, breath coming quick. The Moon ignores them. She touches her fingers to the dead girl's mouth.

It requires a special kind of strength, The Moon says, looking up at last, right at Maycie. Her eyes are still dark and bottomless. To take everything that humans give you, the things they cannot hold even in themselves. She couldn't do it for even one person, how could she do it for all of you?

Goldie stills. You mean because of the drugs? she asks. Because you could just. Not do drugs.

The Moon turns from Maycie to look at Goldie, and although Goldie is expecting reproach she gets condescension instead, which is worse, how it burrows beneath her skin, how it turns *no wonder you're so hungry* into something pathetic, not a joke she's in on but one at her expense.

It is not because of the drugs, The Moon says, scornful. Then she looks closer at Goldie and the image of Henry swims into Goldie's mind as if put there, bloated and stitched together, horrible on the slab. Henry on the bed instead of Jane Doe, Henry floating in the moonlight without his boots. Goldie glares down at them on her feet. She'd found them the next day by the road, as if he'd kicked them off, as if he'd swum to shore and removed them after he fell from the boat. But why would he have gone back into the water? What had he been seeing, so completely off his gourd, that made him leave the safety of dry land?

The coroner said his heart had already stopped by the time the gator got him. He hadn't known he was being eaten. He'd had no idea.

But why had he gone back into the water?

To be human is to be lonely, The Moon says, but less annoyed now, like she sees Henry too, like she hears the question in Goldie's mind. You can't help it. It's at the core of you. That is why you used to pray to me. Only the strong can swallow it and survive.

Swallow what? Harding asks, voice low, and The Moon smiles.

Everything, The Moon says. All the grief, all the rage, all the anguish, all the envy, and still turn the tides anyway, over and over, every day.

So we need somebody who deserves it, and – Jen points at the body on the bed – she didn't. Is what you're saying.

You're very literal-minded, Jennifer, The Moon tells her, but doesn't disagree, which Goldie figures is confirmation enough. Then, slyly, The Moon glances at Goldie and proposes, What about Max? He seems strong.

What's your obsession with my brother? Jen asks, scowling: And also, no, I'm not going to murder him. For one thing, my dad would be pissed as shit.

For another it's wrong, Maycie says.

Yeah, Jen agrees, without conviction. That also.

So it *doesn't* have to be a woman? Goldie asks, trying to redirect the conversation, not caring for the way The Moon keeps shooting knowing looks at her. Jen's unbearable sometimes but she's smart, she'll notice and figure out that something's up and then it will be this whole big *thing* that Goldie doesn't want, has never wanted. It's not like she wants to *hurt* Jen. She *loves* Jen. She'd die for Jen right now, it's just that Jen is annoying as shit.

I mean, if you're suggesting Max, that means it doesn't have to be a woman who replaces you, right? Only, I thought you were like, the Divine Feminine, or whatever.

The Moon laughs, too knowing, and reaches out a hand to stroke the dead girl's face. Goldie realizes that now they have a *new* problem, which is that they have a dead body in the room that's not going to get up and walk itself back out.

There is Divine Feminine in all things, The Moon tells her. Men, women, plants, water. I am a planet, Golden. Gender doesn't operate for me the way it does for you.

Jen says, Not actually a planet, and everyone ignores her.

But *you'd* be okay with being a dude, Goldie presses. Like in your human body. On earth, where people care about that sort of thing.

Not everybody cares, Harding mutters quietly.

Lots of people do, though, Jen agrees, glancing at Goldie like she's said something particularly clever even though all she's done is point out how shit people can be. If we put you into a dude and you walk around being all Divine Feminine this, Divine Feminine that, it'll be a bloodbath. Like that's just the reality of it. We live at the end of the American empire, you're gonna get hate-crimed.

I feel confident that I will be able to handle myself across a diverse array of scenarios, The Moon tells them.

Jen shrugs. Your funeral, she says. Okay. So we need to find someone who nobody would miss and who deserves to be stuck up in the sky doing a shit job until the heat death of the universe.

Goldie thinks about her brother and about Max and about the heat death of the universe and she doesn't want to murder anybody, doesn't think she could if she tried, but she had come into this world holding her brother's hand and maybe she could leave the way he did too. Jen had said *deserves it* but deserves what? Jen *would* think it was a punishment, Jen *would* be so extremely task-oriented but maybe… but Goldie's different. Goldie could do it. Something sparks in her chest at the thought of it, the terror and the joy of terror, the jumping with both feet into the not-knowing of whatever it is that comes after. Jane Doe on the bed in Goldie's underwear.

The Moon is looking at her, knowing, knowing. She gets it, Goldie thinks. The Moon really *gets it*.

Goldie's phone pings.

We're All Gonna Die Party in Bluffton. BYOB., says Max's text. He and Jen both text like that: proper capitalization, full punctuation. *I'll drive.*

Goldie frowns. *thought you'd be mad at me.*

I'm always mad at you. Coming or not? The others can come too.

maybe.

Are you for real, Jen says, exasperated, as Goldie's phone pings. This guy again?

Goldie looks down, panicked, and then remembers, with a sweet sweep of relief: she had saved him in her phone as *maximum ✏️*.

harding

now.
new moon minus six and a half hours

The first thing we're going to have to do is get rid of this body, Jen says, somewhere to Harding's left. She's right, obviously, in that way Jen is often right, which is extremely annoying but undeniably sensible. Harding's not really paying attention to her because Harding is paying attention to Maycie, who is staring at The Moon, and The Moon is staring back, with an expression that says she knows something Harding doesn't.

Mace, Harding murmurs. You okay?

Of course I'm not okay, Maycie snaps, brittle, yanking her arm from Harding's gentle grasp and pressing her hands to her mouth. Everything's so fucked up. Everything's so fucked up. I'm gonna puke. She runs to Jen's bathroom, barely makes it onto her knees before she's spewing chunks. The Moon laughs, not mocking exactly, almost affectionate. Harding wonders what ideas The Moon is putting in Maycie's head. She's been in Harding's head all night saying *Helena Ruth*. Saying *They used to give girls to me*.

Jen sighs and says, Someone go make sure she's not getting puke all over the floor.

I'll go, Harding offers, but Goldie waves her away. No no, let me do it, she insists, and pats Harding's shoulder with some approximation of comfort as she passes. In the bathroom, Harding watches Goldie kneel at Maycie's side to gather her hair back, pulling a hair tie from her own wrist and wrapping it around Maycie's makeshift ponytail.

The Moon is busying herself by running her finger down Jane Doe's cheek, tutting slightly. In the bathroom, Goldie rubs circles on Maycie's back. Harding wants to stop watching but she can't. She's too much, it's always too much, the way she feels, how big and intense it always is. Maycie would – *anyone* would – run screaming from it.

Girls would spend their whole lives sequestered in my touch, dedicated only to me, The Moon whispers into Harding's head, low and seductive. *I could feel it when my light touched their skin.*

There is a surge of desire in Harding's heart at the vision that blooms into her mind, crisp and fully formed, of Maycie tucked away somewhere, drenched in Harding's light, *only* Harding's, always, forever. No one to take her away, not even Maycie herself. Harding's to protect and to cherish and to… to…

Worship? The Moon supplies.

No, Harding says, too loud and too sharp, and it draws a delighted laugh from where The Moon is reclining against Jen's Pottery Barn flower pillows.

No what? Jen asks. You *don't* think we need to handle the body problem?

No, I, of course we do, Harding says, stumbling enough that Jen gives her a very discerning look. I just. Look, can't *you* do anything about it? She turns to The Moon, her hands going to her hips. Can't you be *useful?*

I can be very useful, The Moon promises, and Harding sees it in her head again, Maycie in moonlight that kisses her shoulders. But if you're asking whether I can magically dispose of the corpse you all brought home, the answer is no.

This night is such a mess, Goldie sighs, coming back in from the bathroom to drop into Jen's beanbag chair and glare up at the ceiling. Maycie trails behind. Harding doesn't look at her. Can't. She shoves her trembling hands into her pockets and wishes her dad went in for things like rosaries, but her dad believes ritual is heathen practice. Prayer is all there is, her dad says.

Look, we'll just shove her out the window, Jen decides. Dad's in the kitchen, that window faces the other way. Then we can go down and drive her to the water and push her in. Done.

We can't just *push her in the water*, Maycie says, horrified. The gators—

We'll be lucky if they do, Jen says curtly. No evidence.

Evidence of what?!

Body-tampering, says Jen. She's looking at Maycie like Maycie is stupid. It's illegal to steal a body, Maycie.

Maycie buries her face in her hands. We're going to jail, she moans, and drops to the floor again, curling up at Goldie's feet. Harding goes to sit beside her, tentative, one hand going to Maycie's ankle and resting there, holding on. This is okay. This is normal. This is good, comfort for a friend, Harding giving of herself and not taking of Maycie, The Moon in her head whispering *My light like water, their skin drinking it in.*

There's this party, Goldie says eventually. She holds up her phone. We could go.

Jen snorts, derisive. Now is not the time to be thinking about your popularity campaign, Goldie.

Goldie glances at her, hurt clear on her face for a second before it's quickly replaced with disdain. That's not what I'm saying, dickwad. I'm saying it will be a high concentration of the type of people who would throw and attend an end-of-the-world party, which probably means it's not exactly going to be populated by saints.

They invited *you*, Jen points out. What's that say.

Harding looks at her hand on Maycie's ankle.

Just because people want to party for their last moments on earth doesn't mean they deserve to die, Maycie argues, twisting her foot a little. Harding lets go. She doesn't want to hold on if… she knows how people react to her, how her own awkward solemnity makes them do as she says, fold into her desired shapes.

Harding never tries to manipulate anybody but she somehow does anyway, just by wanting things. It's not a real choice if she's tricking them with the force of her desire, it's… goodness isn't good if it isn't freely given, that's what her dad says, we are tempted *so that* we can choose to deny ourselves. *So that.*

Goldie rolls her eyes. No, you're right. We should instead track down a gang of violent criminals and infiltrate their ranks so we can ascertain the most evil among them.

Maybe we can find somebody who's suicidal, Maycie suggests.

Or who wants it, The Moon says idly, looking at Harding. The power. The devotion. The labor of love.

Yeah, I don't think we can go around asking people if they want to *become the moon*, says Jen, rolling her eyes. Well. I mean Goldie is right that unless we're considering breaking into the jail or something, a party will have the highest concentration of potential candidates.

Not sure I love that terminology, Goldie mutters. They're people.

It's called compartmentalization and some people use it to cope, Jen snaps, then lets out a long breath. Maycie pushes to her feet and goes to stand next to her, resting her cheek on Jen's shoulder. Jen's hand comes up automatically to stroke Maycie's hair like it's Maycie who needs the comfort. Harding feels a swell of dry fondness for her. Jen shudders out a sigh. Okay, look. One problem at a time. First we get rid of the body. She's going out the window, end of.

But— Maycie begins, and Jen squeezes her shoulder, a warning.

It's stupid to risk carrying her downstairs, Jen says flatly. If we get caught the whole thing's fucked.

Jen's right, Harding says. We should... she should go out the window and then two of us can take her to the water.

Harding, Maycie hisses. What about, like, isn't there some religious rule about death, and what you're supposed to do?

Harding shrugs. Not in our denomination. Once she's dead her soul is gone. It's just a body.

The Moon laughs, glittery and pleased. Oh, Helena, she singsongs. You have so much to learn.

Don't call me that, Harding snaps at her finally, flinching. Nobody calls me that.

Somebody does, The Moon whispers into her head, knowing and sly, and into Harding's mind his face swims into view, firstborn of a pastor just like her, studying at Liberty just like her, came down with some volunteers to do a meet and greet with the new South Carolina cohort. Harding's mom had driven her and everybody said *Helena* all night. He'd said her eyes were pretty. He'd said he'd be glad to see her around campus. He had touched her hand and Harding had wanted, viciously, to bite it.

Nice young man, her mother had said. Beaming. *Oh, Helen. Your future is so beautiful.*

Harding takes a few deep breaths. She pushes it away. That's next year. That's later. Harding's whole life. I'll go, she says, itching to get away from The Moon and her temptations, The Moon and her easy way out.

I'll go too, Jen says. We're the strongest and I know this neighborhood best – Mace, Goldie, you stay here and pretend we're, I don't know, researching.

What if Max knocks? Maycie asks.

He won't, says Jen.

But what if he does?

Then tell him to fuck off, Jen instructs, exasperated. Lock the door and don't unlock it. Easy peasy.

Easy peasy, echoes The Moon, smiling.

Jen nods once, that's decided then, goes to the window and opens it. Peers out. When she pulls her head back in she makes a face. Might be a rough descent, she admits. Tree branches.

Harding goes to the bed and hauls the body up by her armpits, then drags her off the mattress with a *thump!* before shuffling to the window.

Everything okay up there? Jen's dad yells up the stairs.

It's fine, leave me alone! Jen yells back. I want to dissolve with a family that's not a fucking nightmare!

Don't say fuck, calls her dad, and then nothing else. Harding imagines what life would be like if she could tell her parents to leave her alone. If she could say fuck in front of them without regretting it for weeks.

Tonight she'd told her dad she was going out proselytizing, to save as many souls as she could before the end of the world, because her dad had looked at the sky and said *2 Peter 3:10: the heavens will disappear with a roar; the elements will be destroyed by fire, and the earth and everything done in it will be laid bare.*

Laid bare indeed, coos The Moon in her head as Jen grabs the body by its legs and together they manage to half-haul her onto the windowsill.

Harding looks down at the body's face. Pretty. Sallow. Some scarring on the edge of her cheek. Sorry, she murmurs, and then, without letting herself stop to think about it, she shoves her out.

They all hold their breath, but there's no call from the kitchen or Max's room; if anyone has heard the body's clatter, they're not asking about it. So Harding and Jen slip downstairs and out to the car, dragging Jane Doe back through the dirt and over the gravel before heaving her up into the trunk.

Harding drives. Jen gives directions. The Moon sits in the trunk with Jane Doe even though there's literally no reason for her to come. Keeping an eye on things, she'd said, looking at Jane Doe with, Harding didn't know. Maybe tenderness.

They're quiet, mostly, til Harding pulls as instructed onto a half-hidden patch of grass, backing in so the trunk faces the water. The Moon has Jane Doe's head in her lap and she's stroking her hair. Harding watches how gentle her fingers are.

The Moon looks up and stares at Harding with her dark-light eyes. She doesn't open her mouth, but Harding hears her say: *Not everyone can bear it.*

Bear what, Harding says out loud as Jen gets out of the car and goes around back to open the trunk.

The intensity, The Moon tells her. Of feeling. But you could, couldn't you? Doesn't your father always say?

Harding flinches as the trunk opens up and Jen says, Dude, what are you waiting for? so Harding gets out of the car and goes round back to help roll the body out, letting gravity bring her to the ground hard. They drag her the rest of the way. At the water's edge they both pause.

Uh, says Jen. I guess we should. I don't know. Say something.

Harding looks over at her, surprised. Why?

Jen shrugs. I dunno. I feel like Maycie and Goldie would.

We're not Maycie and Goldie, Harding says. That's the joy of Jen, to be honest. She isn't emotional the way Goldie and Maycie are. She understands that you have to be practical about your life. You have to do things you don't want to do, that are expected of you, because you live in a society and society has demands to make.

Jen nods. Yeah. It just seems like it's the good person thing to do.

I'm not sure we're that either, Harding says dryly, and Jen laughs. Jen likes to be a we. Harding knows that. Everybody knows that.

S'pose not.

The Moon pokes her head out the window. Chop chop, ladies, she calls.

Bitch, mutters Jen, but she's smiling a little, almost fond. Jen's not scared of The Moon, Harding realizes; Jen *likes* her.

They bend down and roll the body into the water. It buoys for a few seconds. Harding is half-waiting for a gator to come and grab it, but nothing happens; it floats, at first in front of them, and then, gently, away. Harding and Jen stand still and watch.

Water's warm at least, mutters Harding, sort of lamely. She doesn't know what else to say.

Jen hums, thoughtful. You know, a hundred pilot whales mass-stranded themselves earlier this month in Australia. They came up from where they usually live, which is so deep it's hard to study them, and they flung themselves onto the beach to die.

Uh, says Harding. …Bummer?

Nobody knows why pods do this sometimes. They think maybe it's grief.

Whales feel grief?

Everything feels grief.

Is this about your college essay, Harding says.

Jen casts a despairing look in Harding's direction and

shakes her head, sighing a little. I was *going to say*, it's stupid. There's no point in it. In killing yourself for it.

Harding stills, head jerking over to look at Jen. Has Jen been hearing it too? The Moon in Harding's head, making promises that Harding would have no choice but to be sacrificed for?

I'm not— I wouldn't, Harding bites out. The words come automatically: It's wrong to. We're not on our own timetable. God decides when.

Jen blinks at her. Huh?

Maycie's suicide idea. I… things aren't *that* bleak. She tries to make it sound like a joke, like her heart doesn't sink whenever she remembers what's ahead, the endless always of it, Helena Ruth your future is so beautiful.

What? No. Obviously not. Jen hesitates. I'm not talking about that. I'm saying I know you've got a crush on Maycie.

Harding chokes. That's… no, I— *what*?

Jen turns then, gathering Harding's hands in her own. We all might, like, *die* tonight, and it would be stupid for you to get to the end of the line without admitting to yourself that you're a lesbian. And that you don't think God is real.

I do think God is real, Harding argues, just to have something to argue that isn't the other thing.

No you don't, Jen says dismissively. You're too smart.

Yes, I *do*.

Fine, maybe you do, but you don't believe it the way you're supposed to. Jen's voice is a little triumphant, like she's won something. You don't want to go to Liberty, can we at least agree on that?

Harding grits her teeth. Liberty's fine.

Jen's quiet for a minute. Then, inexplicably, she says, They huddled on the surface for a while.

Who did?

The fucking *whales*, Harding, Jen snaps. They hesitated before deciding to strand themselves. They don't usually do that in mass strandings, it's usually totally out of the blue.

Jen, Harding begs. Make some sense.

I'm saying I don't think they wanted to die! I'm saying they had a moment where they were still choosing. This is— this is your pre-stranding huddle, okay? So choose not to beach yourself.

Harding thinks: We are tempted so that we can choose to deny ourselves. And she thinks: Not everyone can bear it, the intensity of feeling. Helena Ruth Harding was named for her grandmother and for the story of Ruth and Naomi, a story her father said of a woman dutiful to her filial responsibility. But Harding doesn't think that's what the story is.

Harding thinks it is a story of those who can bear the intensity of feeling and those who can't. The Lord took everything from Naomi and he did not do it all at once, he took it piecemeal, day after day, slowly, for five years, but when the time came to take Ruth away Ruth said Fuck You. Ruth said I will follow her through the desert and my hands will bleed and my feet will bleed and my stomach will be empty and I will marry a man I could never love half as well as her just to make sure she will always have enough to eat and I will hold her when she dies and I will die alongside her, even if my heart keeps beating, I will be dead, I will be just a body and its functions. Even when Naomi said *Go* Ruth said It's not your decision to make if I love you or not, I love you, I get to decide to love you, I get to decide to sacrifice myself on the altar of loving you, I get to follow you through the desert and if you starve to death I get to do that too. I will love you every second of every day that my dead body continues to move about the world and I will hold onto you until my fingernails are ripped and bleeding and I will keep you alive the way trees do, growing new life on the dead stumps, building forests on their dead, around their dead, *inside* their dead, I will feed your ghost with food from my own mouth, I will never let go, I will *never* let go, I will die still holding on and then we will be dead together, and when we are dead I will be wearing your boots.

There's a soft burbling sound; when Harding looks out at the water, Jane Doe has begun to sink. Her mouth must be filling with water. She floats as long as she's less dense, but as the water gets in and her clothes soak, she'll sink. In a few days she'll probably float back up after the gases start to release. Or something. Harding knows it's float – sink – float.

Around her, somehow, impossibly, is a warm bed of moonlight. When Harding looks back, The Moon is still sitting in the trunk of the car, her head rested in her hands, watching them. But the water around Jane Doe is pale and silky, lapping up against her like a caress. In her head, Harding hears The Moon's many-voiced whisper saying *Helena Ruth. Harding. Don't you want to be both?*

Harding replies, quiet: I don't understand what it is you want from me.

Nothing, I guess, Jen tells her, and Harding realizes Jen

can't see it, the bed of moonlight, the kiss of the water on Jane Doe's cheek. That it's just for Harding, between her and The Moon. Jen lets go of Harding's hands and deflates a little. Do what you want. I just thought *somebody* should say it to you before we, you know. She waves a vague hand.

Harding is fiercely glad that it's Jen here with her, saying it. Awkward Jen with her terrible metaphors, not picking up on Harding's panic, wanting to be done with the conversation as desperately as Harding does.

Although. Jen knowing about Maycie means everyone knows. Jen probably had to be told.

Harding closes her eyes. How'd you know that? she asks eventually, opening them and turning now to look at Jen. About the whales.

Dunno, Jen says on a shrug. Read it somewhere. I've got all this stuff just sort of – she waves a hand at her temple – floating around. Making connections everywhere.

It's hard being smart, Harding laughs dryly.

It actually *is*, Jen grumps. You think I don't know I'm annoying? I can't help it. I know things, I can't just *not* know them.

Harding looks closer this time. Jen is agitated, staring out at the water. I don't think you're annoying.

Yes you do. It's fine. Part of it is probably jealousy, so, it's sort of a compliment really.

That makes Harding laugh. Good old Jennypenny. Insecure and overconfident in equal measure. She feels like Jen has given her something, and wants to return the favor. She says quietly, I… you're right. About me.

115

That you're a lesbian?

Harding rolls her eyes, purses her lips. That I don't want to go to Liberty.

Jen opens her mouth, closes it again. Harding watches her decide to let it go. Okay. You don't have to.

It feels like I do.

Well, says Jen, you don't.

I could become the moon, Harding says before she can think not to, lowering her voice so The Moon doesn't overhear, even though Harding suspects The Moon can hear everything, even the things she doesn't say out loud.

Jen goes quiet. You could, she agrees. I don't— not that I want you to. But. One of us could. And then none of us would have to… you know. She runs a hand across her throat.

Do you think you could do it? Harding asks, and when she peers out at the water the moonlight around Jane Doe flutters, like it's waving.

Jen doesn't pretend not to know what Harding's talking about; she shrugs. I don't want to, obviously. But you can't limit your perspective. If the option is to kill somebody or kill the entire world, it feels kind of selfish to get all emotional about it. It's just the trolley problem.

Trolley problem?

Yeah, you know. There are two tracks, and on one track is one person and on the other track is four, and the trolley is going to hit one of them but you have to pick which.

Just step in front of it, Harding says. To stop it.

Jen hesitates, then turns to look back at the car. It's bright from the inside, lit up. She bites her lip, then turns back to Harding and says: Well. It goes against the premise of the philosophical query, but. I guess you could. I mean, *I* wouldn't. But. She shrugs.

Not everyone can bear it, Harding murmurs.

Harding, says Jen. We were *chosen*. By The Moon. Because we, because she saw something in us. I don't want to kill anybody but it's childish to pretend like we might not *have* to.

Jesus Christ, Jen, says Harding.

Someone has to be clearheaded about this whole thing! Jen snaps. I know it's ugly to think about but not thinking about it won't help anybody. Everybody's acting like I'm a monster just because I'm being a *realist*.

Let's just — one thing at a time, Harding says. Okay?

Jen holds up surrendering hands. Fine. We should get back anyway.

They walk side by side back to the car. Jen drives. Harding watches her from her periphery, her calm hands on the wheel, Jen who knows everything, who isn't afraid to think about it. Jen who knows it's an option that one of them swallows the moonlight, who doesn't flinch from the idea of Harding fleeing her own body, not wanting to live anymore inside it.

yesterday.
(jen)

Look: obviously Jen had some unresolved issues but at least she knew what they were, at least she wasn't pretending she *didn't*, which was really her whole beef with Goldie and Harding. Maycie was an only child which obviously explained almost every messed-up thing about her, but Goldie and Harding were always pretending they didn't have their own family shit going on.

Take this moment, for example: Harding with the knife against her skin, all of them staring at it, Harding's brow a tiny furrow. Harding hated her life more than anyone else Jen knew. One day Harding was going to go fucking apeshit.

Goldie was watching with big, hungry eyes. Curious. Goldie always wanted to know what it was like. 'It' being anything. Everything. If someone else did it first, Goldie wanted to do it second. Never first but always biggest and brightest and loudest. Jen had worked so hard after Henry died to make sure Goldie didn't use him as a blueprint, to make sure she didn't make it through the funeral and then think to herself *that seems fun*. It would be just like Goldie to kill herself out of a sense of FOMO.

So that's why Jen said, I just don't think we should be slashing our wrists in service of a joke.

Harding looked up and Goldie glared at her. Harding said, I'm not going to *slash my wrist*. What the fuck, Jen.

That's a big knife, Jen pointed out, and it's literally directly above where the vein is. Are you stupid?

Harding looked down. Oh.

Oh, Jen mimicked. Christ.

Maybe just do the hand? Maycie suggested.

Will that draw enough blood? Harding wondered, frowning. Goldie said I'm supposed to bleed on all five points of the pentagram.

Cut where the skin bends, Jen advised. So when you make a fist it'll squeeze more out. I don't think there are any critical veins in your hand that you could slice.

So Harding moved the knife up a few inches, held it in her closed palm. Maycie held her breath but Harding was all business. No hesitation, no showboating. She curled her palm around the knife and ripped it back, quick as a starling, and when she flexed back open the blood was pooling in her hand. She walked with careful, deliberate steps, not spilling a drop til she came to one of the points of the pentagram, and then she tilted her palm ever so slightly to the side til the blood trickled off and splashed on the floor.

After – tomorrow – when Jen thought back she'd think that she hadn't felt anything, that obviously nothing had actually *happened*, but for a second, just as the final drop of blood kissed the final point of the pentagram, Jen thought maybe she felt time slow down. She thought maybe she had time, as it fell, to look around at all three of her friends, Maycie with her held breath and Goldie with her hungry eyes and

Harding with the tiny furrow in her brow, and feel so full of love it made her skin hurt, achy and taut like she was going to burst out of it. She thought maybe she could see, in a way Jen usually couldn't – Jen wasn't huge on emotions – Jen's EQ was rocky at best, she knew that, she was well acquainted with her own flaws – she thought she could see them all blown open and laid out before her, all their grief and rage and anguish and envy, a feast that Jen would take into her own body if it would put them at ease, if it would settle the tide long enough for them to row ashore. That's what Jen felt like, that's how intense it was, that's how slow.

And in the back of Jen's head she heard Max's voice saying *Jenny*, saying *Jenny Jenny Jenny* and she felt right before the blood hit the floor that maybe there was a world in which they loved each other again, even if he was a men's rights activist, even if he was an asshole, even if he thought her mom was a slut, because Max was her brother and he'd loved her first, Jenny always pointed toward the world, tide-bound. Jenny in his arms because that's where she was supposed to be.

Harding's blood gasped as it splashed against the hard-wood. Time sped up again. Jen shook her head and knew none of that had been real, that it had been her mind playing tricks, Jen's mind was always playing tricks, that was the trouble with knowing too much. Sometimes you didn't know how to organize everything, so it all came back to you with weird distortions. Jen's heart felt big in her chest. Too big, still. Jen closed her eyes as Goldie smothered the candles and waited for the tide of her own emotions to go out.

now.

*new moon minus five hours
and forty-five minutes*

Harding says, I think we should talk about the worst-case scenario.

They've just gotten back, Jen parking the car on the street in front of their neighbors' so her dad wouldn't hear the engine. They came in through the back door, same as last time, but didn't bother with any sort of distraction for Max. He said, Did you go somewhere? and Jen looked at him with utter disdain and drawled, Go *where*? The fucking *moon's* gone.

In Jen's room, Maycie and Goldie are snuggled on the bed, which makes Harding's stomach do that thing it does whenever she's forced to confront the fact that Goldie had Maycie first, and still has her the most. Harding has her in a different way, special, but Maycie knew Henry – really *knew* him – and something about that has always made them special to each other, Maycie to Goldie but Goldie to Maycie, too. Harding wants to touch Maycie all the time and can't. Maycie touches other people and Harding hears her own thoughts whining. Why. Why. I'm right *here*.

The Moon is sitting on the windowsill, looking up.

Harding looks behind her; she thought The Moon had followed them in, but here she is, impossibly. Well: she's The Moon. Maybe not impossibly. She turns her head when Harding speaks and gives her a knowing look, glancing at where Goldie and Maycie are tangled and then back, raising her eyebrows.

What worst-case scenario? Maycie asks, brow furrowing as she looks up from where she's got her head tucked against Goldie's shoulder, their legs tangled together at the knee. Harding doesn't look. Harding doesn't let herself.

But Harding's been thinking, the whole drive back. Jen's right. About looking at the ugly thing, not flinching away from it. Harding is named for the Ruth who said Fuck You to God when he tried to take her from Naomi. Ruth whose book comes after the bloody history of Judges, of God-honoring slaughter; Ruth whose book leads into 1 Samuel, of God-honoring law. It's a thin line between sacrifice and murder. One's okay. One's not. Harding's mom always says that sometimes the only difference between what shines and what's dull is a little elbow grease.

So she says, Killing somebody.

Better to know how and not need to than need to and not know how, Jen agrees, and Harding's grateful to her, more grateful than she's ever been. Jen gets it. Harding thinks maybe something changed between the two of them, at the water's edge. On the drive home. Jen's unflappable voice saying *You could*, because Jen's practical. Jen can look at ugly things, beached whales and murderous trolleys, and say only *You have to choose.*

I might throw up again, says Maycie, miserably.

Harding reaches out and gently strokes behind Maycie's ear, not able to help it. Goldie gives her a mean look, but Harding ignores it. Maycie likes when Harding touches her. Maycie asks for it.

You're seriously considering this? Goldie asks, staring. Putting someone down like they're a sick animal?

We're all sick animals, Harding says. Before God, she adds in her head. A hundred suicidal pilot whales, she thinks, everything grief, she thinks: Jen's onto something there.

Harding remembers last night, the knife in her hand, the blade against her skin. It was soft, surprisingly smooth. It hadn't hurt when she'd sliced her palm. She hadn't even felt it til this morning, when it was trying to heal, both sides of the cut reaching for each other and wanting to hold tight. She'd flexed a few times just to feel the pull of it.

It's difficult for Golden, says The Moon. Our little sunshine girl. Things always look different in the light.

Shut the fuck up, Goldie snaps at her. Just *shut up*, just—

Harding reaches out and puts her hand on Goldie's head. It's okay, she says. Goldie, it's fine. You don't have to do anything you don't want to.

Goldie's not used to it like Harding is.

In *9 to 5* they thought they'd killed him with rat poison, Maycie suggests hesitantly. We could do that. Surely one of our houses has rat poison laying around.

It would take kind of a lot of rat poison to actually kill somebody, Jen tells her, not without regret. It just feels risky to rely on chemicals. I really think if we're going to do it we're

123

going to have to know it's fatal. I was thinking maybe stabbing, or—I mean, my parents are super anti-gun, do any of you guys have one lying around?

Harding's dad does, but he keeps the bullets locked in a safe she doesn't have the code to. Goldie and Maycie both shake their heads.

Damn, says Jen.

Fucked, Maycie mutters. Fucked, fucked, fucked. Harding's hand twitches against her side so she tucks it into her pocket. She flexes, feels the twist of pain along her life line. It's good, to feel it, the reminder of her body, that her body is trying to heal. That Harding's body wants her to be alive inside it.

The Moon, who has been still and quiet since Harding and Jen came back, lowers her head. She looks directly at Harding.

She's beautiful, Harding thinks. She doesn't have a body, exactly, more a form than an actual corpus, but it's beautiful, smooth at its edges. A dark-light thing. Harding never lets herself look at anybody but she looks now, at The Moon, at the shape of her shoulders, the curve of her hip. The Moon watches her look, smiles, smiles, welcomes it. Welcomes *Harding*.

You can't give me your body by killing it, The Moon tells her, sorrowful, bracing. *But you* can *give me your body.*

Harding sees it in her mind, crisp and clean, Harding with a blade in her hand, Harding at the altar, Judith and Holofernes. Harding and The Moon, their bodies coming together and merging, their bodies heavenly, their bodies cosmic, their bodies made of light.

No more grief, no more shame, no more fear, no more Liberty.

It's a small price, Harding thinks. If she cannot run the knife against her own skin, she can run it against someone else's. What would there be to fear? There will be no heaven for her, anyway. The sacrifice would be giving up whatever comes after this world, would be never seeing her beloved dead again – but the reward would be saving Jen and Goldie and Maycie from it, would be escaping the road laid ahead of her, would be Harding's light on their skin, warm and everywhere. Everywhere. Harding finally allowed to look. Harding not permitted to look away.

Yes, The Moon purrs.

… won't work, Jen is saying. It's too malleable, it won't be anything like the real deal.

Harding blinks. Huh?

A pillow, Jen says, clearly repeating herself. To practice stabbing.

Oh. Right. Sorry.

Get your head in the game, says Jen.

What about the boxing dummy in Max's room? Goldie asks, reluctant. I saw it earlier. In the corner.

Ohh. Jen taps her chin. That's smart, Golds. Yeah. Although I dunno how we'll convince him to let us use it, plus it weighs like a thousand pounds, there's no way we can drag it up the stairs.

Gosh, sighs The Moon. What to *do*.

There's a breath of quiet. The Moon looks at Goldie. Goldie looks back. Harding wonders what they're saying

125

to each other, wonders what The Moon knows that Goldie doesn't want to tell them. After a moment, Goldie sighs. Well, she says.

Harding, Jen, and Maycie turn to look at Goldie, waiting. She taps a finger against Jen's side table, chewing her lip. Well? Maycie prompts. Do you have an idea?

It's just. If we can't get it out of the room, we'll have to stab it *in* the room.

Not sure Max will be thrilled about that, Jen laughs. He's obsessed with that thing.

Yeah. So he can't also. Be in the room.

Goldie, Harding says, as patiently as she can, if you're building to something, please get there. We don't have all the time in the world.

Secrets, secrets, sings The Moon.

Can you chill, Goldie snaps, and scrubs at her forehead like she's got a headache. Okay. I just. I didn't want it to come out like this. You guys have to promise to be cool about it. Because like, if you really consider how things are, this is like, *so* not a big deal. Given the surrounding circumstances.

Goldie, Harding says.

Fine! she cries. Fine. I'm fucking Max.

First there is absolute stillness, and then The Moon tosses her head back and laughs, a long, delighted peal of laughter that shakes the house. Maycie squeals and scrambles off Goldie's lap like she's allergic to it; Harding catches her by the arm and reels her in, wrapping both arms around her middle, tucking her face into the bend of Maycie's neck and inhaling. She doesn't care if anyone sees. Harding's decided. Last night on earth. She doesn't care what anyone thinks. She bites down and Maycie goes near-limp, relaxing. Oh, she says, sounding slurry.

Jen is staring at Goldie, frozen, her mouth cracked open. Goldie is looking back, her chin raised, her jaw set. Stubborn.

Max, Jen repeats.

Yes, says Goldie.

Max Max. My *brother* Max.

That's the one, says Goldie.

Okay. Jen's voice is calm. Define fucking.

Goldie hesitates, clearly caught off guard. Uh. Fornicating?

The Moon laughs again. The Moon is clearly having a great time. She brings her knees up and rests her chin on them, beaming. It's cruel, Harding thinks, but The Moon is old and never had anyone to teach her kindness. Harding can do it differently. Harding can do it better. Harding's future is so beautiful.

No, Golden, I mean what are the *parameters*. Ongoing? Frequent? Exclusive?

Goldie blows out a long breath, shrinking into herself a little. She plucks at Jen's comforter, glancing at Maycie and Harding and then down again when she receives no help. Ongoing. Occasional. Not exclusive.

Right, says Jen. Fine. One more question.

Shoot.

Are you *demented*? Jen shouts.

Goldie flinches, and Maycie says sharply, Jen. Don't.

Don't what? She's fucking my brother! Jen yells, pointing at Goldie like she's Goody Proctor. Her hand catches the edge of her shelf and the vase Jen's been guarding all night topples off, shattering on the wood floor. Jen stares down at the shards, mouth going tight, wobbling at the edges.

I'm *civilized*, mocks The Moon.

It's okay, Maycie soothes, ignoring her, pulling away from Harding just enough to extend a hand toward Jen and smooth it down her arm. I know it's— I know, but given the demands of the moment, we have to be rational, okay?

I *am* rational, Jen snaps, still staring at the shattered vase, but then takes a deep breath, breathing out long and slow, closing her eyes. It was a smart thing to say, Harding thinks. Most of the time Maycie shoots straight, but she has this inside her too, Harding knows. Clever and demanding and sneaky, getting what she wants without having to ask for it.

Goldie says, I'm sorry. I should have told you.

No, Jen says, you shouldn't have *done it*!

It's not a big deal, Goldie mutters, mutinous now, folding her arms across her chest. I'm allowed to fuck whoever I want. It's called sex positivity, sorry none of y'all are feminists.

So you'll take Max outside and fuck him while we practice stabbing his boxing dummy and then you don't have to help, Jen surmises. Typical. We do all the hard stuff while Goldie gets her rocks off.

I said from the jump that I'm not going to murder anyone, Goldie tells her flatly. I haven't changed my mind. At least I'm still being useful.

Goldie, you don't have to— we can think of something else, Maycie says placatingly. Maybe Max will want to go to that party?

Goldie winces again, this time with guilt, and Jen cries, Oh my God. He already knows about it. He's motherfucking Maximum Pen Leg.

Knee, says Goldie, reflexive. Maximum Pen-Knee. Penny. As in—

I get it, Jen snaps.

This is why I didn't tell you. I knew you'd get all *Jen* about it.

I think it's a good idea, says Harding. Goldie and Jen turn to look at her; Maycie adjusts so she's tilting upward, leaning more heavily against Harding's chest. Looking up. Harding's own earthshine. Harding lets herself bask in it, then goes on: Goldie gets Max to drive her to the party, we stay here and practice. She can scout out someone and we can meet her there.

Like bait, Jen says.

But I've been searching from morning, sings The Moon. For my golden hen.

Goldie looks at Jen. Jen looks at Goldie. Maycie burrows backward like she wants to disappear inside of Harding; Harding holds her tighter. Harding wants that too. Harding wants them to be so close that there is no Harding and no Maycie, there is only the light of their bodies, there is only the warmth of their light.

Jen's face is blank, hard; Goldie's, searching. Harding doesn't know what she finds. If she finds anything.

But Goldie says, Yeah. Okay. I'll find someone.

Someone who… the Moon said Jane Doe couldn't handle it. Maycie says it with her eyes on Goldie, gentle but firm: She said it was a punishment.

No, Harding interrupts. She said it was something not everyone *deserves*.

Same thing, says Maycie.

It's not, Harding answers. She looks at The Moon, and The Moon is beaming at her. The Moon is looking at Harding's body like she will be glad to be inside it, when Harding no longer is.

Goldie's smile is wide and sharp, a dagger of light in a darkened room. She says, Don't worry, Mace. I'll be sure to pick someone who really sucks.

maycie

now.

new moon minus five hours

Goldie texts Max and everyone is quiet while they wait. Jen is sitting on her bed, toying with a piece of the broken vase, not looking in Goldie's direction and when she does, looking through her. Erased. It's spooky, almost, Jen's ability to white out what she doesn't want to see, but it's effective, too. Maycie thinks if Jen had yelled more, had been shitty more, Goldie would have been relieved. She's never been good at being ignored; Maycie can see it getting to her by the way she's fidgeting.

Harding's hand tightens where it's come to rest possessively on Maycie's hip. Maycie stays perfectly still. She doesn't know what's come over Harding, what happened when she and Jen took the body to the water. But her shoulder aches where Harding bit it, pleasant and tingling. The Moon keeps looking over at them, pleased and quiet, keeps watching Harding with a kind of hunger that freaks Maycie out. She burrows more deeply into Harding's arms, supposes they're just doing this now, supposes there's no point in being secretive when they're all probably going to jail tomorrow for murder anyway.

Goldie's phone vibrates. She picks it up. He says he's ready, she says flatly, and stands. It's sort of awkward, even for Maycie, even though it's not *her* brother Goldie's been fucking.

Which— look, of course Goldie is, of *course*. Maycie doesn't know why anyone's surprised; Goldie always does the thing that will hurt the most.

You'll need clothes, Maycie says, struck suddenly by Goldie in her tiny pajamas, Goldie in her dead brother's boots. Her heart pinches, achy and sour. You can't go dressed like that.

Why? Too slutty? Goldie sneers, and Maycie doesn't think anybody else hears it but there's tears at the bottom of the words, sloshing around the edges.

No, Maycie tells her, disentangling from Harding, ignoring Harding's unhappy sound. You'll just look insane turning up in pajamas and combat boots.

She probably won't wear them very long, Jen mutters, and Maycie hears herself snarl Jennifer, shut your fucking mouth.

There's my earthshine! cries The Moon, so pleased she's nearly smug. Then, into Maycie's head, she adds: *That's my Maycie in the moonlight. Maycie taking a dead man's boots.*

Jen's mouth snaps shut, eyes going wide as she stares at Maycie. Goldie stares at her too. The Moon is right about this, Maycie thinks. Neither of them ever think that Maycie can be strong. Neither of them ever stop to think that maybe Maycie is nice because she's *decided* to be, not because she has no other choice.

It's easy to be an asshole when the world sucks. Maycie is stronger than either of them, Maycie is the one who sees things as they are and chooses to be better instead of sinking down into the gunk. People look down on kindness but you have to be really strong to choose it consistently, to choose it even when you want to scream, to choose it even when no one else ever does. You'd have to be really strong to do all that and turn the tides over anyway, over and over, day after day.

Only the strong can swallow it, The Moon had said. Maycie gets it. Maycie *gets* it. Maycie swallows and swallows and swallows.

Maycie takes a deep breath. Sorry. Just— shut up, okay? Goldie, c'mon, you know I'm right. We can get Max to drive us to my house first, you can borrow something. Then you guys go on to the party and I'll bike back.

Goldie hesitates, then gives in. Okay. Yeah. You're right.

Great, Maycie says, and she crosses over to take Goldie's hand. She doesn't look at Jen and doesn't look back at Harding even though she can feel Harding's eyes on her, can feel Harding's longing like a string around her wrist. She tucks Goldie's hair behind her ear. Let's go downstairs, okay.

Maycie chances a look at The Moon. She's beaming.

They go to Max's room first. He's waiting at the door with his keys in his hand and ignores Maycie to give Goldie a once-over. Hello again, Golden, he says, low and smooth, and Maycie thinks privately that he's probably practiced it, looking at himself in the mirror.

Maxie, coos Goldie, in a voice Maycie's never heard her use before. She sounds like The Moon. We've got to swing by Maycie's first. I want to change and I can't run into my parents or it'll be a whole thing.

Maycie manages a smile for Max. I'm not gonna come to the party, she tells him.

Max shrugs, unbothered, and they go out to the hallway. They don't have to sneak this time – he ducks his head into the kitchen where his dad is and he says, Hey, I'm gonna drive Goldie back to her house. Her parents want her home and she's too anxious to drive.

His dad looks up, frowns, hesitates, then says, Well, all right. But come straight back.

Will do, says Max.

And Max, says his dad, tapping his finger on the table. You seen Jen in a while? She okay?

Max laughs. She's Jen, he says.

Yeah, says their dad, rueful. Okay. Drive safe.

The three of them trek out to the car, Goldie and Maycie holding hands, Max out front. Both Maycie and Goldie climb into the back, and Max doesn't say anything about it, maybe not that surprised. Maycie doesn't know. It's not a long drive to Maycie's but it's pretty quiet, Max tapping his thumb along to the radio, Goldie staring blankly out the window. Maycie tries to imagine what it's like between them, when it's *just* them, whether Max is sweet, whether Goldie likes his company. She knows Goldie likes to hurt herself with her choices but she wonders whether the hurting always hurts, or if it's like when you eat too much and it only hurts in the after.

Maycie has known Goldie for a long time. Maycie grew up alongside her, watched her and Henry, watched her afterward, shriveling away to nothing, all delicate bones and perfect dusky skin. Watched her appetite dwindle and her laughter get too loud.

When they get to Maycie's, Goldie leans forward and presses a kiss to Max's cheek. Thanks, Maxie, she murmurs, and even in the dark Maycie can tell that Max is flushing pink. Yeah, he agrees. Whatever. Be quick.

Beauty takes the time that beauty takes, Goldie tells Max, singsong, and then she's slipping out of the car and Maycie is following. She pauses with her hand on the door, not yet getting out. Goldie always treats her like she's young, like Goldie is her benevolent big sister, but it was Maycie who climbed down into the oyster bed and took her dead brother's boots and it was Maycie who snuck food onto Goldie's plate when she wasn't looking, who sat with her beautiful hair held between her hands when Goldie threw all the food back up. Maycie knows how Goldie wants to love her and so she lets herself be loved that way but Maycie remembers Henry, eyes hazy, leaning into Maycie and whispering *Goldie's spirit is so fragile* before he laughed and darted away, and at the time she thought he'd just gone crazy but now she thinks he was probably right. High as a kite, and right all the same.

Maycie doesn't know who gave Henry drugs the first time but she thinks that if she ever found out, she would kill them. She would. She really, really *would*, gentle Maycie with a blade in her hand.

In her head, The Moon's many voices say, *I am strong. I am strong. I am strong.* Maycie hears her own voice in the chorus. Maycie lets the other voices drop out. *I am strong*, says The Moon as Maycie. *I am strong*, says Maycie as The Moon, and doesn't shiver.

Max, Maycie says, and he looks at her in the rearview, raises an eyebrow. If anything happens to her while she's with you tonight. Whether it's your fault or not. I will blind you with my fingernails.

Max blinks, visibly surprised. Uh.

I will take a chunk out of your jugular with my teeth, Maycie tells him, calm. Calm. Henry in the water. Maycie with a blade in her hand. I will put your dick through a spiralizer.

Dude, what the fuck, says Max.

I will reach down into your throat, says Maycie, and I will pull your guts up out of your mouth. Got it?

Max is gaping at her in the rearview, face pale. Maycie thinks: You have no fucking idea how strong I am.

Max says, Jesus. Yeah, I got it.

Great, says Maycie, and hops out of the truck and onto the grass, dark where the moonlight should be. When Maycie lands, the grass lights up with the reflection of the footlights on her white sneakers. Earthshine, she thinks.

yesterday.
(goldie)

After, when they'd cleaned up the Winter Room and climbed back down the ladder, they'd leaned up against the covered porch and Goldie had made more horrible cocktails and they'd piled into Maycie's mom's bed, all wrapped up in each other even though it was so hot and the fan didn't do anything but move the air around. Maycie's house had made its weird oozing noises and Harding had lit a candle and Goldie had thought, you know, you know, all the other stuff was crap. There was just this: the bed, everyone's limbs belonging to everyone else, the heat of their breath, the intensity of how it felt to be hollowed out like this, with only room for Goldie and Maycie and Harding and Jen, just the four of them, breathing the same air, thinking the same thoughts. Goldie could feel the cut on Harding's hand as sharply as if it were sliced across her own, she could feel the dizzy spin of Jen's drunk thoughts, the too-fast whirl of knowing so many things and not being able to parse what any of them meant. She could feel the steel in Maycie's spine, the spikes she hid beneath all her softly petaled roses, the razors of her teeth. For the first time in a long time Goldie felt *hungry*, like she could eat a whole cow, she could eat a whole *person*, that's what it felt like, that's what being best friends felt like, that's what being a girl and having best friends felt like, cannibalism, all of you at the feast and of the feast, all of you taking parts of each other without even realizing it, becoming each other as you became yourself, jealous of the pieces of yourself the others took but proud of them too, proud that they'd been deemed worthy and edible, proud when you were closer to being fully consumed than anyone else but also furious that anyone else would dare to take any piece of you, the pieces you'd grown so painstakingly, that you'd put together from all the things you stole from everybody else, you were only you as long as nobody else was but of course everybody was everybody when you were best friends like this, there *was* no you, there *was* no them, there was only GoldieMaycieHardingJen, one person, one entity, breathing. It was their right to be hungry. It was their right to eat. It was *only* their right, and that was it, wasn't it, that was the real thing, that was why Goldie hadn't told Jen about Max: because it wasn't Goldie's right to bring Max into it. Harding and Maycie's whole thing was okay because they were part of it, part of each other, part of everything, they could hurt each other and they could love each other but *only* they could do it, only *they* were allowed. The second you let somebody else in it was ruined, it was over, Goldie knew it, Goldie understood then that she was the one who had broken them, someone always had to break it when it was good like this and it was Goldie for them, Goldie who hadn't meant to but perhaps had, too, who was always chasing something, who was never happy with how good it was now when there was something else that might taste better, when

140

there was something else that might hurt worse. Goldie had fucked Max and kept fucking him and now she could see it, clear as a movie, clear as the moon in the sky, the future laid out before them, four paths that never crossed again, not like this, not a woven braid. They'd leave the island and they'd never look back except to think of each other and wish they were together, would keep the memories of tonight and all the other nights tucked away, precious and breakable, and they'd maybe be happy and they'd maybe be successful and they'd maybe have lives they'd look back on and be proud of but they'd never, *never* be as real, never as fully alive as it was possible to be in Maycie's falling-down old house in a bed with your three best friends, still young, still hungry, still flayed alive on the altar of being a girl. You couldn't ever get your girlhood back because it never existed as something that was yours, it always belonged to the people in bed with you, a shared experiment, a creature you raised only to slaughter with your own two hands.

now.

new moon minus four hours

When they get inside the empty house, Maycie doesn't turn on any lights and Goldie doesn't either. They go up the creaky stairs and Maycie lights a couple of candles and Goldie strips down to nakedness, standing in the middle of the room. She holds her arms out, almost helplessly, waiting for Maycie to put her together, a paper doll in a windless room.

Maycie understands. She reaches out and tangles their fingers together and leads Goldie to the bathroom, knowing what is needed, knowing what's being asked of her, even if Goldie doesn't. Goldie never knows what she's asking for. Maycie always knows what to give her anyway.

Goldie gets into the shower and Maycie gets in with her, washes her hair, scrubs her shoulders, bends down and soaps behind her knees, leaves her shining. They don't speak. It's understood. Maycie has always belonged to Goldie but Goldie has always belonged to Maycie too. It was Maycie with Henry in the water. It was Maycie who removed his boots. Even if Goldie doesn't know this in its factuality she knows it in her body. She knows it in how she bows her head and lets Maycie scrub the shampoo through it.

After, Goldie sits on the edge of Maycie's bed and Maycie

blow-dries her hair. She curls it, stands close, holds the heat to Goldie's head but doesn't burn her. Goldie burns herself enough; Maycie will always use gentle hands. She presses her fingers against the crown of Goldie's head. Goldie melts into it. Maycie feels holy, feels that Goldie is holy, not the sacrifice but the offering, not the victim but the altar itself.

When Goldie is dry, she looks up, eyes wide and un-adorned. Maycie thinks she looks more like a movie now than she ever does all done up. Maycie has always thought Goldie was beautiful but with an edge of jealousy to it that seems dissolved and pointless now, leaving only Goldie beautiful in the halo of the candles in Maycie's bedroom.

She does Goldie's makeup, careful and precise. Her hand doesn't shake as she smears the lipstick, as she flicks a line of eye-liner across Goldie's lids. She feels the reality of Goldie's body, the weight of her lashes, the wrinkle of her mouth, the awkward edge of her eyes. She dabs perfume to Goldie's wrists and neck and behind her ears, gives a spritz to her hair because it holds scent the longest. She dresses Goldie in a sweet sunshine-yellow dress that falls to her knees, almost modest except that Goldie's tits are bigger and show more at the garment's mouth.

Maycie crouches down until they're of a height. She waits til Goldie meets her eyes. They look at one another, not speak-ing. Maycie can see it, even without The Moon in the room to put it in her head: Goldie's hurt and fury, Goldie's belief that nothing, once broken, can be fixed. Maycie has known Goldie. Maycie had known Henry. Maycie takes Goldie's hands in her own as if this could keep Goldie from chasing after whatever it is she is always running toward.

Soft earthshine spills out from Maycie's feet and illuminates Goldie like a stage light. Maycie feels a kiss on her shoulder. She waits for The Moon to speak but there's nothing; just the pool of light. They look down at it together.

Who will you choose? Maycie asks.

Goldie shakes her head. I don't know.

Liar, says Maycie, and Goldie closes her eyes. I know you. You want to choose yourself. But it won't work. None of us will do it if it's you.

Jen might, Goldie says. She was pretty fucking mad.

Maycie sighs. She takes Goldie's chin in her hand and stretches upward. She presses a kiss to Goldie's lips, chaste and gentle. I love you. Nothing is beyond fixing.

There is a long pause while Goldie just looks at her. The light from Maycie's feet is warm and yellow. Goldie says quietly, What do you think it's like? Being the Moon?

Maycie thinks about it: the endless spinning eternity of it, the cold, the distance, all the painful longing humans send you, with no hope of reprieve. She thinks about watching boys die in water. You would have to be strong. You would have to be stronger than everyone else.

Fucking awful, Maycie says. You'd suck at it.

Goldie smiles. Hey. How come you wanted Harding and not me?

It's asked teasingly, but Maycie thinks there's real curiosity behind it, and she laughs. You're my best friend, she says. I couldn't love you more even *if* I wanted you.

But have you ever? Wanted me?

No. Maycie smiles. I want to be you. I want to eat you.

Sometimes I want to shove you off a cliff. I love you.

Yeah, Goldie agrees. Yeah, exactly.

Nothing is beyond fixing, Maycie says again.

This time, Goldie is quiet. She chews her lip. She's beautiful in Maycie's reflected light. She's beautiful in every light. Not a streak of sunburn on her. Fifteen minutes on each side. Even. She says, I always wondered why he took off his boots before going back into the water.

Maycie holds her breath.

If he'd managed to drag himself to shore, why did he go back in? Why did he take his boots off first? It never made any sense. Goldie looks over at the corner of the room where she shed her clothing. Henry's boots lie discarded alongside everything else, one upright, one toppled over on its side. I think the answer is that someone found him.

Goldie looks back at Maycie. Maycie lets herself be looked at and says nothing.

I think someone found him in the water and dragged him onto land. I think they took off his boots before the gator got him. I think they saw him dead, really dead, the dead he was before he was just a body, you know what I mean? There's a period of time when you die where it's you but dead, before you become just a corpse. I didn't see him til after but someone did, and they took his boots off, when he was still Henry. When they were still his boots.

Maycie knows what Goldie is saying. Maycie thinks this could be the right time to say it out loud. *I saw him in the water.* But what would it do for Goldie except hurt? Only the strong can swallow it. Only the strong can take it in, take it

145

all in and hold it so other people don't have to, other people with smaller hands. So instead of the truth, Maycie murmurs, So what?

So one day we'll all just be bodies. One day the sun will explode and we'll all be even less than that.

Climate grief, says Maycie, dry.

Everything grief, Goldie says.

Maycie feels it in her heart, the everything grief, the fullness of it, the eruption from beneath the skin, Goldie tearing herself away from the being that is the four of them, the creature of GoldieMaycieHardingJen, and it won't be MaycieHardingJen afterward, it can't be. It's all or nothing. It's four or zero. Goldie made a critical error with Max and she's determined to make more because of course she is, of course she would, that's Goldie, that's always *been* Goldie. When she learns how not to hurt herself she won't *be* herself anymore, not *this* version of herself, not the version in GoldieMaycieHardingJen. To become that person she has to rip herself away. She has to kill herself to become herself and to kill herself she has to kill them, too. Maybe that's it, Maycie thinks, maybe *that's* the sacrifice, maybe *that's* why The Moon chose them, not because they were broken beyond fixing but because they were too good, they were too strong together so she had to pry them apart. The thing that dies isn't whatever body they manage to arrange for her; the thing that dies is the four of them. The thing that dies is who they are to each other.

Of course Goldie would want to offer herself as the sacrifice, but she never actually could. None of them would be able to bring the knife down, not even Goldie herself. Never in a million years. But: Maycie glances out the window, where Max is waiting. Goldie looks too. Max honks once: *I'm waiting.* Max is the interloper. Goldie had no right to bring him in. Goldie has to be the one to cut him out, Goldie with a blade in her hand. Someone who really sucks.

I love you, Maycie says again, a goodbye. I knew you first.

You knew Henry, Goldie agrees, and kisses the bone beneath Maycie's left eye, as delicate as light glancing off the water.

Outside, Max honks his horn again.

Okay, Goldie says, and rises, bright as the sun.

now.
new moon minus three hours

Maycie bikes back to Jen's house and goes in through the back, straight to Max's room. She has no trouble seeing. Moonlight spills out ahead of her feet. Jen and Harding are already there, Harding with a blade in her hand. Jen with that stupid broken vase shard rolling over and between her fingers. They're standing close, really close, and something ugly and hot flares in Maycie's belly. They've been all chummy since they came back from getting rid of Jane Doe and Maycie doesn't know what changed while they were doing it but she hates it, hates how close they're standing, hates how Jen mutters something and Harding throws her head back and laughs.

What's so funny, Maycie demands, stepping into the room, and Harding says, oblivious: Jen.

Jen! Jen's famously *not* funny, Jen's the stick-in-the-mud, Maycie loves her but Jen sucks, everyone knows that. She glowers at them and Jen looks over and then *Jen* laughs and says, Every once in a while I'm capable of making a good joke, Mace.

I'll believe it when I hear it, Maycie says, and marches over to Harding and squishes herself up against her and knows that time is running out and doesn't care that Jen is there and throws her arms around Harding's shoulders and kisses her, hot and a little mean, a little mad, *fuck you*, you're *mine* to love, you're *mine* to kill someone with, to dispose of a body with, to hold onto, mine.

Whoa, okay, Jen says, and Maycie hears it distantly but isn't really listening, is paying attention only to the way Harding's mouth feels on her own, the hunger in it, the fear, the blade of the knife in her hand pressed up against Maycie's back, careless and sharp.

Maycie bites Harding's lip until she tastes blood and then she pulls away. She turns to Jen. Chin out. Glaring. The room is so bright it's almost hard to see.

Jen holds up both her hands. Okay, she says, easily enough. Mace. Okay.

Maycie's heart slows down. She breathes out, shaky. Harding's hand – the one not holding the knife – closes around her hip. Good. Good. Maycie feels soothed. That's where it should be. Maycie is Harding's. Harding is Maycie's. Maycie wishes the knife had cut her. She wishes she'd have a horrible scar. She asks: Where's The Moon?

Jen shrugs. She said she didn't want to spoil the show by watching the dress rehearsal.

Harding leans in, nuzzles her nose behind Maycie's ear, runs her hand up Maycie's side, beneath her shirt. Goldie on her way?

Maycie nods. She's gonna be fine. I told Max if he hurt her I'd claw out his eyeballs.

Jen blinks at her, surprised. And he believed you?

I meant it, Maycie tells her. So yeah, he believed me. She

turns to look at the boxing dummy. She thinks about how it had felt in the car. *Pull your guts up out of your mouth.* She could do it. Maycie thinks she has only just begun to realize the extent of what she's capable of. She says: Okay. How are we doing this?

Well, Jen begins. Jen has her Lecture Voice turned on. If whoever it is sees the knife they'll probably try to run away, right?

Right.

So two of us will have to hold him.

Three of us, Maycie says. We'll have Goldie back.

Jen doesn't say anything. Maycie knows. It's okay. She knows. She had anointed Goldie with perfume. She had said goodbye. Acute time pressure. Everything grief.

Harding says, Three of us. Yes.

Google says there are seven lethal places to stab somebody, Jen says, reading from her phone. The spinal cord, the carotid artery, the armpit—

The *armpit*?

That's where the axillary artery is. So then there's the lungs, the liver, the femoral artery—

Isn't that like. In the dick? Maycie asks, her hand floating instinctively down to cover herself.

It's in the groin area, says Jen, prim. *Near* the dick. Oh, this one's good, it's the popliteal artery, which is right behind the knee. One of us could bend down and pretend we're tying our shoe or something. Easy peasy.

Easy peasy, Maycie repeats, and it tastes weird in her mouth, like someone put it there when she wasn't looking.

Well, our dummy doesn't have knees, Harding points out, so we can't really practice that. Should we try the others, just in case?

Jen nods. She holds out a hand for the knife.

Harding frowns. Why're you the one doing it?

Oh, says Jen. I just assumed. Because you're religious and Maycie is...

Hey, Maycie protests. I could do it.

You've thrown up twice just *thinking* about it, Jen points out.

Yeah, but that was before, Maycie says.

Before what?

Before I understood, Maycie thinks but doesn't say, knows she can't say, knows it's her job to know and keep pressed against her chest. Only the strong can swallow it. She says: Before I realized there's no other options left.

Do you *want* to do it? Jen asks, sounding genuinely puzzled. Because you don't have to. That's all I'm saying. Only one of us has to do the actual stabbing so there's no reason why—

And Maycie thinks none of you know me, none of you know shit about me, you love me how you want to love me and I've always let you but I'm the strongest of all of you, I'm the one who holds onto everything, I'm the only one Goldie calls when she's drunk and stranded and I'm the only one who Jen calls when she's fighting with her mom and I'm the only one Harding can stand to look at with desire and I'm the one who holds all of you together in my hands and they're sore and they're tired and I'm going to develop arthritis and

151

I'd do it forever but I won't get the chance because you're all determined to ruin everything, nobody's competent enough to do it except for me, to keep the tides going in and out.

Maycie snatches the knife from Jen's hand and pulls away from Harding's tender grip and she jams the blade into the dummy's neck, right where the carotid would be, and there's no blood but she knows there will be, she's ready for it, she takes the knife out and stabs it back in again, this time in the spinal cord, the armpit, the lungs, the liver, and then low on its belly, just above where the dummy ends, the closest she can get to the dick that isn't there, she shoves the knife in and buries it as deep as it can go and twists until the fabric or plastic or whatever it is makes a horrible ripping sound and she yanks the knife out and tosses it on the floor and turns to face them both and she says There. Done. It doesn't have to be such a big fucking *production*, and then before she can say anything else Harding is on her, hands on Maycie's jaw, yanking her inward, kissing into her mouth and backing her up against the wall and Jen is saying Oooooooookay I'm just gonna... Harding is sinking to her knees and picking up the blade and running it across her hand, across the unhealed cut from yesterday, and Maycie is sinking down in front of her and holding her own palm out and it doesn't hurt, it feels smooth and sweet, and then they're clasping hands together and their blood is mixing and Maycie feels it, feels Harding blending with her in a way that's forever, that's permanent, that can't be taken out or changed even if they never speak again.

I love you, Harding says. Maycie. I—

Shut up, Maycie snarls. Don't. You're going to, in the fall you'll be at—

No, Harding promises, no, I won't, I won't be, I promise, I've got a plan now, I know how to get out of it, I know how to be with you, forever. I know.

Maycie presses her hand to Harding's face. There's a smear of blood when she takes it away and it settles something furious and violent in Maycie's chest and opens her heart up too, opens it like a mouth. She says, I saw him. Henry. I was alone and I saw him in the water. I'm the one who took off his boots.

You weren't alone, Harding murmurs, ducking in, burying her face in the curve of Maycie's neck. You're never alone in moonlight.

No, Maycie snarls, the moon is never alone with *me*. She's been lonely and angry and hungry and now she has *me*.

Harding says, I know. Earthshine. I know.

No matter what, Maycie tells her, choked, tears spilling down her cheeks as fast as Harding can swipe them away. No matter what happens. You're my blood now. Harding. She swallows. *Helena*.

Harding goes still. That's not me.

Yes it is, says Maycie. It's a part. Even the moon has its phases.

They look at each other.

Helena Harding bows her head.

153

now.
new moon minus two hours

Goldie knows: Maycie was right. If Goldie lay herself on the altar, none of them could do it. No one would take the offer, not even Jen. Not even fucking Max had broken them beyond repair, not really; Goldie hadn't fucked Max to hurt Jen, she'd done it to hurt her*self*. Jen would forgive her. Jen is already trying, can't help herself.

Behind her, in the backseat, The Moon crosses and uncrosses her legs. She reaches forward and runs her fingers through Goldie's hair. Goldie leans back into the touch. Goldie lets The Moon ripple through her, lets the image float into her head, Henry in a ring of moonlight, floating in the water, held by her, unflinching, never looking away even as his face filled with bloat, even as all the life went out of him, as he became nothing but the house Henry used to live in, nothing but a body and its functions. He wasn't alone, not at all, not ever, not any of the times he had snuck out and come back with that dazed look about him, sweet and pliant, climbing into Goldie's bed and letting her hold onto him as he slipped away. She never tried to stop him, she knew better. She *knows* better. You can't hold on to a thing that wants to leave. You can't hold together a thing that wants to break. You can't stay still on a planet that has to spin and you can't look away from it either, you have to swallow all the grief, all the rage, all the anguish, all the envy, and still turn the tides anyway, over and over, every day. You have to turn the tides. That's what Goldie knows that Maycie doesn't know, that Harding doesn't know, that Jen doesn't know. You can't keep them from going out. No matter how much you want to, no matter how much the water wants to, no matter how tightly the waves might cling to the shore.

Henry died and Goldie can't because her friends love her in a way nobody loved Henry, not even Goldie herself, who had loved him more than anything else.

Goldie has said this whole night that she won't kill any-body. But Goldie knows what her friends don't know, and she is not naive enough to think that nobody has to die. If she wants it to be herself then she will have to do something worse than fucking Max, something worse than lying about it, something bad enough to sever GoldieMaycieHardingJen forever.

The Moon makes a soothing sound. All things die, Golden, she murmurs. Henry knew it. I think you know it too.

Max says, What are you looking at? and Goldie smiles, touches his shoulder, tells him, feeling sick: Nothing. You.

now.

new moon minus one hour and forty-five minutes

Is Max back yet? Jen's dad asks with a puzzled frown.

Jen twirls Harding's car keys in her pocket. Nope, she says, and pops the P. He texted. Got a flat. I'll go pick him up.

Her dad hesitates. That's her dad for you. Believes in independence for kids. Believes in treating them like adults. But hesitates when you tell him something, prefers to be asked.

Jen says: What, you'd rather he walked back in the dark? It'll take ages. And there's no moon. He'll get himself killed.

S'pose you're right, her dad says finally. Okay. But straight home. No detours.

Will do, says Jen.

Her dad goes back into the kitchen. Jen and Maycie and Harding go out to the car. Jen gets in the driver's seat because Harding sliced her hand back open and so did Maycie, whatever, Jen guesses that if it might be your last night on earth you've gotta shoot your shot, good for them. Maycie and Harding aren't the problem.

Fucking Goldie. Fucking *Max*.

Jen types the address Goldie texted them into her Google Maps and they drive in silence. Harding and Maycie are in the back, Jen's alone up front, but not alone, The Moon beside her, crossing and uncrossing her legs. Watching Jen with that same knowing smile.

You're my favorite, Jenny, The Moon says, and when Jen glances in the rearview Harding and Maycie are curled up in each other, not paying attention. They can't hear me. It's just us. I wanted it to be just you and me.

Why, Jen asks without speaking out loud, and The Moon smiles wider, pleased that Jen has understood, that Jen knows not to pop the bubble they're in.

Because you're the pragmatic one. You're not *afraid* of it.

Of what?

Looking at ugly things head-on.

Jen stops at a red light. She waits. She looks at Harding and Maycie in the rearview; The Moon nods in understanding. They can't do what you can do. They're too young still. They're too emotional. But you see things as they *are*. You're not afraid to make the difficult decisions. You're not afraid to do the difficult things.

Jen pauses. Harding, Maycie, and one not with them. The Moon watches Jen steadily, and Jen knows they're both thinking the same thing, Goldie deciding who deserves the burden of becoming the moon, Goldie in the car with Max. *Someone who really sucks.*

Could you do it? The Moon asks. Kill your brother to save your friends? To save the world?

Is she going to pick him? Jen asks, bracing herself. If she is, no point in flinching from it. Better to know now. Better go in with her eyes open.

The Moon shrugs. Dunno. Humans are funny. You never know exactly what they're going to do. That's why I'm asking you.

Jen thinks about her brother. About how much she used to love him, and how little she can manage now. She thinks about the tour guide saying *they flirt too much with death*. She thinks about *virgin first time rough sex raw secret*. About 'DON'T GET CAUGHT / FUCKING MY LITTLE SISTER'S VIRGIN BEST FRIEND RAW ON MY SISTER'S BED'. It looks different now, that video, those search terms, now she knows that it's sort of true, that part of it is, that part of what he'd liked was the deception, was the going behind Jen's back, the having one over. Max fucking Goldie isn't about *Goldie*, Jen thinks, not *really*, it's about *Jen* – not that Max wants to fuck Jen, he just wants to *beat* her, to win, to undo whatever loss he suffered when their dad got Jen's mom pregnant, he wants to go back in time and make their dad change his mind, change his behavior, change his choice, but he can't do that so instead he has to make sure Jen knows that she was a mistake, that she's not anything but an interloper in his family.

But *Max* is the interloper, Jen thinks. GoldieMaycie-HardingJen.

Yeah, Jen says, out loud. *Only the strong can bear it.* She keeps her eyes on the road. I could do it.

now.

new moon minus one hour

When they pull up, Goldie is standing on the lawn in front of the house in a yellow dress. She looks beautiful. Harding gets out of the car and when she gets close enough she can tell she smells like Maycie's perfume. There's no one with her. Harding looks around, thinks that maybe she's knocked somebody out and stashed them somewhere, but when Goldie sees them her lips tremble and then go hard and still. She lets them come to her without moving. She glows in the glancing light from the house's windows, music filtering through.

Where's Max? Jen asks.

Goldie says, He's inside.

I told you— Maycie begins, and Goldie shakes her head.

I know. You were right. It's not me.

And then there's the sound of a car pulling up and a voice from behind them says, Oh, dope, your friends are here. Y'all ready to go?

Harding turns and her stomach plummets. Goldie's eyes are bright and glittering. Beside her, Maycie lets out a quiet, resigned sigh. But Jen makes a small sound, flayed open, and her hands clench into fists as she spins back around to look at Goldie. Fuck you, she says. Why. Goldie. *Why.*

You guys coming or what? Six-Pack asks, leaning out the window, impatient.

We're coming, says Goldie, not looking at him.

You have to be sure, Maycie tells her, stepping into Harding's side, and Harding doesn't understand, still.

We have to turn the tides, Goldie says. She looks at Maycie, then Jen, then Harding, and a tear falls down her cheek: We *have* to.

Okay, says Maycie.

Okay, says Harding.

They turn to look at Jen. Jen is looking up. There's a pinprick of red beneath her chin. She holds herself very still and she clenches her fists and then she scrubs roughly at her eyes and turns toward the car and says, Yeah. We're coming.

Now

Mimi's is empty and dark when they arrive. Six-Pack flicks the light on. He reaches beneath the counter and pulls up five beers, cracks them open, hands them out. They take them. They drink in silence. He's talking about how he doesn't even like to cook but he's gotten used to it, funny old place, Mimi's, the wildest people come through, but the pay is good and he's saving up for a motorcycle, he was gonna do like a *Motorcycle Diaries* kind of thing before the moon disappeared. You know *The Motorcycle Diaries?* Jen asks, can't help herself, she never can, and he laughs and says, Yeah I mean it's pretty famous and Jen's like, Ha. Yeah. I guess. They drink their beer. Harding's hands are shaking. Maycie's heart feels small and skittish, a wounded animal hiding in her ribs. Goldie's stomach hurts, Goldie's feet feel small in her dead brother's boots. Jen watches Six-Pack and thinks about a different version of this summer where she'd fucked him before she went to Yale and never thought of him again.

Now

The Moon stands behind Six-Pack, beaming, dousing him in light, making his skin warm and shiny, and The Moon is saying in four voices, in *their* four voices, The world was always going to peel you apart. You were too powerful as a single breathing thing and so you had to be destroyed. That's how it is. That's how it's been since the days that they sang hymns to me. *With my hands outstretched and with a full heart I bow to the moon.* You thought nobody saw you in the moonlight, but I am the moonlight, and I did. I always do. Always.

Now

Jen is thinking I don't want to kill anybody but it's childish to pretend like we might not *have* to and Harding is thinking I can't give her my own body by killing it but I *can* give her my body and Maycie is thinking only the strong can swallow it and Goldie is thinking no wonder I'm so hungry, grief is cosmic, Goldie is thinking about the line in her college essay that she hadn't asked Jen to write that said *The thing about life is that sometimes the hardest part is just deciding to stay alive* & how she'd read it & cried because Jen loved her so much & understood her so well & Goldie is thinking about herself saying I'd be sooooo cute as the moon.

She says Let it be me.

She says Guys listen let it—

but Jen is taking her hand and squeezing it, Jen is looking at Goldie and there's forgiveness on her face, for Max, for everything, even for this, Six-Pack in Mimi's and the knife on the counter. It punches the breath from Goldie's lungs that Jen could love her still, that Jen could love her so much even Goldie's most pointed hurts aren't enough to kill it. No Jen says; no says Maycie; no says Harding & she reaches onto the counter & grabs one of the cooking knives & Six-Pack says what d'you need that for? & Harding is thinking no more grief no more shame no more fear no more liberty & she's raising her hand up & Six-Pack is saying hey what are you doing & Harding's hands are shaking Harding knows how to give The Moon her body but then Harding is looking at Maycie and Harding doesn't want to touch her only as light, Harding wants to use her hands. Harding's body wants her to be

alive

inside it

Now Jen is watching Harding pause &

she thinks It should be me *I'm* the responsible one *I'm* the grown-up *I'm* the one who can do difficult things *I'm* the one going to *Yale*. She thinks she understands now that the sacrifice isn't the dead man it's the act of killing him, it's the part of yourself that you give up when you bring the knife down, the Moon has never cared who gets killed the Moon cares about who does the killing & so Jen knocks the knife from Harding's numb grip & reaches into her pocket for the vase shard she's still carrying & looks at Goldie and says I'd rather let the whole trolley burn than let it touch you & stabs the porcelain right into the neck, right into the carotid, Six-Pack lets out a yell & Jen doesn't look away from him doesn't look away, there's blood everywhere, on Jen's hands on Goldie's yellow dress on the counter behind him as he collapses to his knees & everyone is screaming & Jen thought she was rational pragmatic but she feels sick & dizzy & scared, he's clearly so confused, she doesn't feel powerful or strong, she feels like her mother. She wants her mother. It takes a few tries, it's hard, he tries to scramble away even as he loses so much blood & she tries to make it quicker by stabbing him again but it doesn't work, her hands on the shard are too slippery & she can't hold tight enough without cutting herself open & even when she cuts herself open he dies so slowly & Jen thinks I'm sorry I'm sorry I'm sorry, The Moon in the background, beaming, The Moon is saying Oh Jenny, you always did surprise me but I'm glad it's you who can hold all the bitterness and the love, who can do terrible things and still hold the world together, Jenny there's blood all over your hands, and The Moon is growing bigger & bigger & Jen is closing her eyes & The Moon says, I'll look up I'll spend a lot of time looking up oh Jenny you'll be such a beautiful Moon & Jen feels herself

e x p a n d i n g—

later.

Goldie orders a beef stroganoff for dinner. She's already two drinks deep when Maycie and Harding arrive, spotting her at the back of Veselka and coming toward her with a wave. Maycie's got on this huge backpack; she's scheduled herself an overnight layover so they can do this before her flight to Argentina. Harding's not carrying anything. She's cut her hair, buzzed in the back. She's wearing jeans and a flannel shirt, even in the muggy September heat, still humid in New York. Goldie's new friends say it'll stay that way til almost October if it's anything like last year. She bagged out on College of Charleston, bagged out on college at all. She's been modeling for an agency up here, living for free in this studio her mom's friend owns.

She stands. It's a little awkward, the hugs, but it would be more awkward not to do it, so Goldie gives one to Maycie and then one to Harding and then they're sitting down together and drinking their sparkling water not speaking while they wait for their food and then Goldie says, So um. Did you guys come together?

Maycie and Harding look at each other and then away. Maycie gives an uncomfortable laugh. Oh – no. Just ran into each other at the door. I'm staying at the airport Hyatt.

I came in on the Megabus, Harding says. It's not a bad trip from DC. Handful of hours.

That's good, says Goldie. Traffic?

Nah. Not too bad. Plus they've got pretty reliable Wi-Fi.

Oh. Great.

They sit quietly again. There was a time when they were never quiet. But it's different now. The group chat has been dead for weeks, been dead since that night, since Six-Pack got blood all over Mimi's and everything got bright and weird and then the moon was back in the sky, beaming.

It's weird to be the only ones who know what really happened, Maycie blurts out, then claps a hand over her mouth. Sorry. I know we said we wouldn't talk about it again. But. It's just been—

Weird, Harding agrees.

Yeah. Goldie taps her nails against the table. I guess we got away with it.

Doesn't feel that way, Maycie mutters as their food arrives. I can't even look out the window at night without feeling sick. I don't know if I want her to be up there or not.

Goldie looks down at her beef stroganoff. She takes a bite just to have something to do with her mouth that isn't a scream.

Have you— I mean, I think you were the last to leave, Maycie goes on. Did you… see…

Goldie shakes her head. I talked to Max, she admits. Right before I left. I just. I wanted to… I don't know. Be sure, I guess. That it really wasn't Jen anymore. But he said she'd basically come home and packed her stuff and driven to Yale and they hadn't heard from her since.

They sit in silence. Maycie makes no move to eat; Harding

pushes her potatoes around. Goldie folds her napkins into funny shapes. She has spent a long time trying to untangle who was guilty of what. She has spent a long time trying to figure out what the right thing was supposed to have been.

Maycie buries her face in her hands. It's all so fucked, she mutters. All of it is just so fucking... *fucked.*

Harding reaches out, almost automatically, and touches the back of Maycie's hand, then freezes, staring at the spot where their skin connects. She pulls back. Maycie looks up at her and smiles tightly, almost more of a wince, then looks back down at the table. They sit without speaking. Maycie's right, though, it's fucked. Goldie had woken up the next morning and not been able to think about her friends without wanting to be sick. She had burned Henry's boots and told her mom she wanted to travel before going to school and her mom had said Okay and sent her to Paris for a month and Goldie hadn't called Maycie or Harding, hadn't texted, had known that it was better that way, that it was the only choice, really, when you thought about it. She'd heard from her mom that Maycie had started her trip early, backpacking some hiking trail, lost in the woods, no cell service, no one around for miles and miles.

I went to Noah's funeral, Harding tells them abruptly, and both Goldie and Maycie turn to look at her with matching puzzled expressions. Harding sighs, says: Six-Pack.

Six-Pack's name was Noah? Goldie asks, surprised. That's. I don't know. It doesn't suit him.

Harding gives her a dry look. Not sure I'm one to judge on that particular issue, she says. His parents are members of the church so my dad did the eulogy. The Moon was there. In Jen's body, I mean. Nobody else saw her but I think she wanted me to. She was wearing a Yale sweatshirt.

Yikes, Goldie mutters.

His mother hugged me and thanked me for coming. She said he. Harding swallows. She said he always spoke really highly of me. He said I was a good tipper. I can't get that out of my head. I haven't figured out what else to do except rip my whole life up. I went home and told my mom I'm at *least* a lesbian and moved out that night. I didn't see anyone else. They haven't... nobody's reached out, so. I guess she told them.

Harding, Maycie murmurs.

It's okay, says Harding. It's... yeah. I mean. It'll be okay. I'm working at this bar in DC. In a few months I might enroll in some classes at Georgetown. I just have to figure out finances. You know.

Yeah, says Goldie. If you need help, uh—

No, Harding says flatly. It's supposed to be hard.

Goldie puts her hands up, a surrendering gesture. She doesn't know what she'd have to really offer, anyway: she doesn't think her parents will pay for Harding to take classes, and it's not like Goldie has any money of her own. Sometimes Goldie doesn't feel like she has *anything* of her own; even her life is a gift from Jen – the real Jen, not the thing in Jen's body – and not one she particularly deserved.

They talk a little, here and there, as they eat. It doesn't feel like there's much to say. Everything that comes out of Goldie's mouth sounds trite. *How are you, how's work*, fuck off. They killed a person. They sacrificed their friend. They'd loved each other so much it went cosmic. Goldie doesn't want to talk about it, and doesn't know how to talk to them about anything else.

Goldie finishes her food and pays the bill. They walk out together, making their way slowly toward the train. Somehow, outside of the restaurant, the silence feels easier, less tense. Maycie grabs Goldie's hand and holds it, gives a squeeze when she glances over.

When they get to the station, they stop and stand facing each other. Goldie drinks them in, both their faces. Beloved, still. A part of her, still, but not hers anymore. Not hers ever again. She thinks this will probably be the last time she sees them. She thinks this will probably be the last chance she has to love them, so ferociously, so wholly and completely and alive.

Well, Goldie says.

Yeah, says Harding, and takes Goldie's other hand.

Yeah, echoes Maycie, and reaches for Harding, the scars on their palms lining up as they clasp hands. They don't say anything else. They look up at the darkening sky and there she is, fixed as always, never looking away. A new moon.

waning crescent

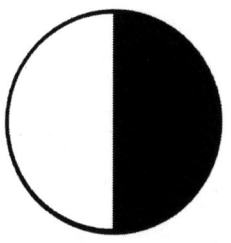

third quarter

waning gibbous

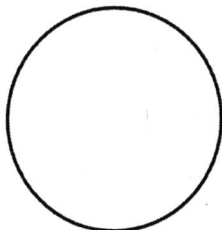

full moon

waxing gibbous

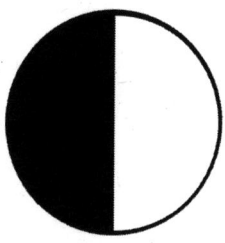

first quarter

waxing crescent

new moon minus zero minutes

New Jen looks up from the book she's reading. Fernando Pessoa, *The Book of Disquiet*. She's laying on a blanket on the quad, stretched out like a happy cat. She loves this body. She loves being alive in it, human and singular. It's so small, down here, so small that it makes everything inside it feel so large. Old Jen had taken it for granted; New Jen loves it.

Sometimes New Jen feels a flash of regret for poor Old Jen, but it is happening less and less as time goes on, as this body becomes more and more her own.

New Jen looks up because someone is gesturing at her, at his ear. He wants her to take her earbuds out. She's annoyed by this. She's reading. She wants to be left alone. She's been sweating all day because it's so fucking *hot*, was it always hot like this? Had it always been? Old Jen had said *shit ass time to decide to come be tied to the fate of humanity* and New Jen hadn't really believed her, but every day her phone warns her about extreme weather, air quality and heat and riptides, constant. She burned her foot stepping on the asphalt a few days ago. Unreal. Still, New Jen is learning how to live in the world from the ground up, so she takes one earbud out. What? she demands, and he frowns.

I just wanted to say I think you're really pretty, he tells her. Are you a new freshman? He sits down next to her without being invited. He leans into her space. She wants to scoot away but doesn't, feels like she'd be giving up important ground if she did. He's bigger than she is, taller, broader; she's never felt small before. She's never felt *too* small, not even in the early phases, because as the moon she was always her whole self, obscured. But now he leans over her and he's grinning like he expects her to grin back. She feels something in her chest, her heart speeding up, she doesn't know why. She hasn't fully gotten the hang of the body and all its functions. He says, My name's Ted, and then he plucks her book from her hands and starts flipping through it, then reads from the inside of the cover jacket: To Noah, from Jen. Who are Noah and Jen?

She looks up. The moon hangs low in the sky, dim still in the dusk. Sometimes New Jen feels like it's lower now than it was before, that when Old Jen became the moon she was sorry enough to drag the whole orbit closer. It must be torture, New Jen thinks, to watch your old body make new choices. It must be torture not to be able to look away.

I'm Jen, she says. And I was reading that.

This is pretty heavy stuff for a freshman.

Yeah, well, I'm very smart, Jen snaps, yanking the book back.

Ted laughs, unbothered. I'll bet. Hey, what're you doing later? A couple guys I know are gonna throw a party, wanna come? Usually it's a no-freshman thing, but. He winks. You're very smart.

Right, says Jen, caught up short. The sun goes down a little, hitting them different. Ted's shadow stretches over her, blocking the light. She looks up at the darkening sky. What would Goldie do, she wonders; or Maycie or Harding or—

Jenny, says Ted. Jennypenny.

She shakes her head. Just Jen.

Okay, Just Jen, are you in or not?

Even the moon has its phases.

I'm in, Jen says, and blows The Moon a kiss.

new moon

Acknowledgments

I want to thank Leah, who is always right in a way that causes me problems; Maartje, who leads my bucket hat study group; Corinne, who knows all the ferry times; and Jessica, whose text notifications are nearly always a threat. I also want to thank my agent Alyssa for her endless patience, my family for their indulgence of my terrible personality, Sarah for everything, Montana for everything else, and Rita, who is a dog. And of course, I want to thank all my best beloveds whose personalities, speech patterns, and jokes I've cannibalized throughout the years. I feel very full.

WE HEXED THE MOON

MOLLYHALL SEELEY

First published in 2025
by Weatherglass Books

Copyright © 2025 Mollyhall Seeley

A CIP record for this book is published by the British Library

ISBN: 978-1-0687941-1-7

Cover design: Tom Etherington
Typesetting: James Tookey

Printed in the U.K. by TJ Books, Padstow

www.weatherglassbooks.com

Weatherglass
Books